CHARACTERS

A Greenwich Village Fable

BY WILLIAM COLLINS

The contents of this work, including, but not limited to, the accuracy of events, people, and places depicted; opinions expressed; permission to use previously published materials included; and any advice given or actions advocated are solely the responsibility of the author, who assumes all liability for said work and indemnifies the publisher against any claims stemming from publication of the work.

All Rights Reserved
Copyright © 2023 by William Collins

No part of this book may be reproduced or transmitted, downloaded, distributed, reverse engineered, or stored in or introduced into any information storage and retrieval system, in any form or by any means, including photocopying and recording, whether electronic or mechanical, now known or hereinafter invented without permission in writing from the publisher.

Dorrance Publishing Co
585 Alpha Drive
Suite 103
Pittsburgh, PA 15238
Visit our website at *www.dorrancebookstore.com*

ISBN: 979-8-8868-3426-0
eISBN: 979-8-88683-406-2

CHARACTERS

A GREENWICH VILLAGE FABLE

Dedicated to Walter "Dede" and Frances Lavorgna Collins

"In nature, a watering hole is like your local tavern. Sooner or later, residents from all over the neighborhood end up there. Like the watering hole, most come to drink, others to hunt. Some are just passing through, and others come to linger..."

"Burnzy's Last Call"

CHAPTER ONE

"So, I'm bangin' this three-fingered midget in the back of the bus yesterday...." I smiled, hearing that line I'd heard a hundred times before, and knew that Danny Pope was in the house. The 'house' in this case was Wilson's, a neighborhood bar in Manhattan on 27th St. between 6th and 7th Avenue.

I rarely travel outside the comfort zone of my Greenwich Village neighborhood anymore. In fact, my friends joke that I think I'll get a nosebleed if I go above 14th St. Venturing up to 27th is an adventure for me these days, but I'd spent the entire day inside doing what the whole country had been doing for the past eight months —watching the OJ Simpson trial. By the end of the afternoon, I decided I needed to get out of the house for a while and ended up at Wilson's. I was watching a couple of guys shoot pool and working on my second Jack on the rocks when I heard Danny's voice.

I like Wilson's. I'll come here sometimes when I need a break from Characters, the dive bar on 6th Avenue in the Village where I sling drinks four nights a week. Since Characters is only a block from my apartment on West 12th St., I usually find myself hanging out there the other three nights of the week as well.

Proximity to my apartment was the reason I first began to drop into Characters, but as time went on I found myself increasingly drawn to the place. Each night brought some new drama to witness, usually directly related to the large amounts of alcohol and cocaine being consumed there: Everything from a shakedown or mugging in the bathroom by a neighborhood punk, to those nights when the whole place would just explode.

People, who just moments before had appeared sane and rational, were suddenly wielding pool cues and beer bottles as weapons while bar stools flew across the room. It reminded me of those big saloon brawls you used to see in old Hollywood Westerns. When I was a customer, I found it exciting and entertaining. Once I started working there, not so much.

When the bartender at Characters got fired after getting into a fight with Paula, one of its owners, I was offered the job by Sal Milano, its other owner. His choice surprised a lot of the regulars at the time. Characters was, after all, a rough scene, and by then had acquired the reputation of being a "drug, thug, and gun bar." I was a 5'6", 130-pound gay man, and a lot of people wondered if I was up to the job. As it turns out, I was.

I spotted Danny Pope leaning against the wall on the other side of the pool table. At 5'10", with a mop of sandy brown hair and the face of an altar boy, Danny looks younger than his 32 years. His boyish look sometimes results in someone making the mistake of underestimating him. It's a mistake they don't make twice.

Circling around through the crowd, I came up behind him, slipped my hand between his legs and rubbed his inner thigh.

Without turning around, he said, "Whoever it is, I'm gonna give you just two hours to stop doing that...."

He looked over his shoulder, and when he saw me his face split into a big Kool-Aid grin. "Was that you?" he asked, turning around. "Yeah, but hey," I answered, showing him my palms, "my hand never left my wrist..." He laughed and said, "You are so lucky I didn't just turn around swinging." "I wasn't scared," I told him. "I knew you'd like it."

Throwing his head back in mock outrage, he demanded, "Who's been talkin'? Jeez, you suck one dick, and all of a sudden you're a fag!" He laughed again and I laughed with him, thinking Danny Pope was probably the last person in the world I'd call a fag.

Danny and his younger brother Teddy were neighborhood legends. Their dad had been in the Westies, an Irish American organized crime gang. The Westies had been responsible for racketeering, drug trafficking and contract killing, and for years had operated out of the west side neighborhood of Manhattan known as Hell's Kitchen. According to Danny, their dad's association with the Westies ended abruptly when the gang found out he'd stolen the merchandise from a truck they'd hijacked and tried to move it on his own. He ended up in a sealed oil drum at the bottom of the East River.

The way Danny explained it, after they seal somebody in the drum, they shoot holes into it so it sinks when they drop it in the river. The more you've pissed them off, the fewer holes they put in the barrel. That way, the barrel sinks that much more slowly, giving the poor bastard inside time to contemplate the error of his ways. If they decide to be more humane, they riddle the barrel with bullets, so it sinks quickly. I think they liked Danny's father. Of course, I also think that if they put that many bullets through the barrel, chances are pretty good that whoever's inside is probably going to be dead before the barrel even hits the water. But what do I know?

"What's up?' I asked him. "I'm trying to get something," Danny said. "I swung by the bar, but Miguel wasn't there yet, so thought I'd try here…"

Miguel is the in-house coke dealer at Characters, something almost every neighborhood bar has these days. He usually shows up about 10 o'clock and hangs around until closing, discreetly selling 20- and 50-dollar bags of coke to the clientele. Most of them usually hang out after they score and spend the rest of the night playing the jukebox, drinking, shooting pool, playing darts and, fortuitously for me, spending money. And, of course, taking regular trips to the bathrooms to do blow.

"You know somebody here who's selling?" I asked Danny. He tilted his chin in the direction of the pool table, where the two players had just racked the balls for another game. "Yeah, right there. Alex." I looked over at the two guys chalking their cues. "He told me he's not holding tonight, but check it out —"

'Alex' was bending over the table now with his back to us, ready to do the break. As he bent over, I saw the top of a plastic baggie sticking out the top of his back pocket. I looked at Danny and raised my eyebrows.

"You see that? Motherfucker lied to me," he said quietly. "What are you thinking?" I asked him. He tilted his beer bottle up and drained it before looking at me. "Why don't you go wait for me up by the front door?" "Okay, sure…." I said, uncertainly.

Danny flashed a smile at me, and said, "Go on, I'll be right behind you.

I got to the door and turned around just in time to see 'Alex' swinging his pool cue at Danny's head. Danny ducked, and the cue struck the head of the guy standing behind him with a resounding smack. That guy let out a roar and pounced on Alex, and then Alex's pool buddy jumped in with fists flying. The other guy's friends started throwing punches, and within seconds the entire room erupted into a full-scale bar brawl.

I felt someone grab my arm. It was Danny, pulling me toward the door. "C'mon, we gotta get outta here before the cops show up!" he shouted. "Dude, it's just a bar fight-" "No, it's not just a fight," he said. He held up a sandwich bag half full of cocaine for me to see. "Now it's a robbery!"

Before I could react, Danny grabbed me and pulled me out the front door. "C'mon," he yelled, "hurry up!" We ran toward 7th Ave. and reaching the corner, he flagged down a cab. Before it even came to a complete stop, he pushed me into the back and piled in behind me. "Take us down to 14th," he told the driver, then leaned back and settled into the seat. As the cab sped down 7th Ave. I looked over at Danny.

"What the fuck just happened back there?" I asked. He looked at me. "Well, the prick bent over to take a shot and I pulled the baggie out of his back pocket. He turned around and told me to give it back." "Yeah...?" I said. "And...?" He smiled. "I looked at him, all innocent, and told him I didn't know what he was talking about," Danny replied. "I said, 'I found this on the floor, and I know it can't be yours, 'cause you told me you weren't holding!' "

I started to laugh. "Dude, you didn't tell him that —" Danny's grin grew bigger. "Yeah, I did!" "And that's when he swung at you...." "Yeah, and hit Big Tony from the balloon store," Danny laughed. "Ha, I wouldn't want to be in Alex's shoes right now." He leaned forward to speak through the partition. "Let us out here on the right," he said to the cabby.

The cab pulled over and we got out on the corner of 14th and 7th. Danny led me to the wooden door of a bar set into a recess of a brick building. We entered, and as the door swung shut behind me, I looked around. Five wide steps led down to a long narrow room, A bar extended down the length of the room on the right, and a pool table and jukebox occupied the left side of the space. It was quiet. Four guys were shooting pool, and another guy and a girl were sitting at the end of the bar closest to the door. They all seemed to know Danny and waved as he walked in. I followed him down the stairs.

Danny walked all the way to the other end of the bar, where a lone drinker sat with a beer, and seated himself next to the guy. He pulled the baggie out of his pocket, swiveled on his stool to face the room, and waved it in the air. "Hey, everybody," he yelled. "Lookee here! Free lines! Come on over and grab a straw!" With that, he turned back around, emptied some of the baggie onto the bar, and started cutting lines.

The lone drinker sitting next to him had frozen with his beer bottle halfway to his mouth and was looking at him. Danny, feeling the guy's stare, looked at him. "What?" he said. The guy stared back. "I'm a cop," he said. I froze.

Danny stopped cutting the lines and looked at the guy for a beat. Then he smiled, lifted his head, looked down his nose and imperiously proclaimed, "Then you don't get any!" He turned and went back to cutting the lines.

The cop continued to stare, as Danny ignored him and stayed focused on his task. After almost a minute passed, the cop gave what can best be described as a bemused shake of his head. He drained his beer, put the bottle on the bar and threw some bills down after it. Taking one last look at Danny, he shook his head again, got up and left the bar, going up the stairs and out the door. Danny turned to me and grinned. "See how much fun you can have if you go above 14th Street?"

CHAPTER TWO

If I had to pinpoint exactly when it all started, I'd have to say it was the afternoon they finally reached the verdict in the OJ trial. I'd worked at the bar the night before and had gotten home to an empty apartment sometime past five in the morning. My friend Jeremy, a pop singer turned actor who was staying with me, was out of town on location, shooting a TV-movie in South Carolina. He'd be gone most of the month.

I took a long, hot shower and ordered up breakfast from Joe Jr's., the coffee shop located downstairs on the corner of 12th St. and 6th Avenue. Within an hour of it being delivered, I'd finished eating, smoked a joint, and fallen asleep in the living room in front of Katie Couric and the Today Show. At some point I must have roused myself enough to turn off the television.

I slept heavily and longer than I'd intended, and when I finally woke up it was almost 4:30 in the afternoon. Stiff from sleeping on the couch, I stretched, splashed some water on my face, and made a cup of tea. I thought I'd run downstairs to grab a paper and a sandwich to bring back and eat in front of the TV. 'Live at

Five,' the local NBC newscast with Sue Simmons and Jack Cafferty, would be on soon.

Once I hit the street though, I changed plans and decided to drop by Characters instead, figuring I could catch up with Diane, the daytime bartender. I see her three or four times a week when we do the shift swap, but we don't really get a chance to talk. Since the bar is usually empty during the daytime, I like to drop in now and then just to shoot the shit with her.

But today, when I got to Characters and walked through the door, I was surprised to find it unexpectedly crowded. Every seat at the bar was taken. More people stood behind those who were seated, pressing up against the backs of the bar stools. All eyes in the room were on the television mounted near the ceiling at the end of the bar closest to the door. I could see it was turned to a channel showing the OJ courtroom, and even though I couldn't hear the volume, I didn't need to. Listening to the conversations going on around me, I knew I'd just missed the reading of the verdict.

I couldn't believe it! I'd watched almost every single hour of the damn trial, and here I'd missed the climactic moment? I was pissed! Based on the reactions I was hearing all around me, other people were just as angry, but for a different reason. The jury's verdict was neither expected nor popular. OJ had been found not guilty!

I could see Diane raging and pacing back and forth behind the bar. Too far away to hear her, I could see her mouth going nonstop in what I assumed was a profanity-laced tirade. I knew her well enough to know she was probably railing against OJ in particular, and all men in general. Diane's the kind of gay woman who's more about the feminism and the politics than the sex.

In her early 30s, she was dressed today in her usual attire of jeans, work boots and a crew neck sweater. I've never seen her wear makeup, and her straight brown hair is parted in the middle and hangs loosely to her jawline. She might be considered pretty, were it not for a certain hardness in her features,

I went behind the bar and approached her. "Honey, are you okay?" I asked. I've seen Diane eviscerate other men who've made the mistake of calling her that. I knew I could get away with it, partly because I'm gay (gay guys get away with a lot of stuff like that); but also, because I have a genuine affection for Diane, which she reciprocates. Usually.

"No, I'm not okay!" she snapped. "I can't fucking believe that that wife-beating bastard got off!" "What's going on here?" I asked her, indicating the crowd. "Where did all these people come from?" Diane grabbed a mug and went to pour a draft beer. "As soon as people heard that the jury reached a verdict, they just started streaming in off the street looking for a television." She pulled on the tap and it started to sputter and spit. "Oh, look at that! Dammit! Now the keg's empty! Fuck!"

"Hey, hey," I said, "Relax. I'll go down and tap a new keg for you." I poured a shot of Hennessey into a glass and handed it to her. "Here. Drink this and take a deep breath, okay?" Taking the glass, she downed the shot and exhaled heavily then handed the glass back to me. "Thanks." she said. "I'm fine." She gave me a half-smile. "Would you mind tapping the keg for me though? That'd be a big help...."

"Of course," I told her. "I'll be right back." "Good," she said. "there's somebody here I want to introduce you to." Diane turned back to her customers. I wondered what this was about. In all the time I'd known Diane, she'd never introduced me to any of her friends. Well, I'll find out soon enough, I thought, shrugging. I came out from behind the bar and headed downstairs.

CHAPTER THREE

The basement of Characters was used mainly for storage. Untapped kegs and cases of bottled beer were stacked in the center of the room. In the far-right corner sat the empty kegs waiting to be returned, and a half dozen empty steel oil drums. Every time I saw the oil drums I thought of Danny and Teddy Pope's father and the fate he met inside a similar drum.

The kegs currently in use were in a large walk-in cooler beneath the stairs. I tapped a new keg and rolled the old one out of the cooler to place with the other empties. As I headed back to the stairs, I heard a voice calling, "Diane, is that you?" Following the voice to the other side of the basement, I found Paula sitting at the desk nestled against the wall. A tiny, nervous woman, Paula is in her mid to late-50s and looks every day of it.

"Hey, Paula, it's me," I said. "I had to tap a keg for Diane." Paula was the co-owner of the bar along with Sal Milano, but only Paula's name was on the liquor license. A felony conviction in Sal's past prohibited him from legally owning a bar. To get a liquor license he partnered up with Paula, who'd been running and owning bars in Greenwich Village since the '60s. To the customers, Sal was the public 'face' of the bar. Paula remained happily in the background, out of sight.

Opened in front of her on the desk was what looked like an accounting ledger with a green binding. It matched the nine or ten other ledgers sitting on the shelf above her head. I noticed a few travel brochures for Florida strewn across the desktop as well.

Even though I'd been working at Characters for over a year and a half, I rarely saw Paula. I only worked nights, and she only came into the bar during daylight hours. Sal told me that she was afraid to come into her own bar after dark, having heard stories about what went on there. One night a couple of customers wanted to play darts, but I couldn't find them in the drawer behind the bar where they were kept. When I asked Sal about them, he told me that Paula took the darts because she was afraid they could be used as weapons by 'the clientele'. Everybody at the bar had a good laugh over that. We all knew that most of 'the clientele' carried their own weapons and would have no need for the comparatively non-lethal darts.

"What's going on up there?" Paula asked. "Is Diane busy?" "Yeah," I told her. "You've got a pretty good crowd." I saw a flicker of concern crossing her face. "We do? What kind of crowd...?" I laughed and said, "No, it's not that kind of a crowd. Don't worry. These people all seem pretty normal. They just came in looking for a television set to watch the OJ verdict."

"Oh, yes, OJ..." she said, her voice trailing off. She began gathering up the travel brochures. "You going on vacation?" I asked, indicating the brochures in her hand. "Umm... What?" she said. She looked down at her hands as if puzzled by what she was holding. I wondered if she was medicated or just distracted and even ditzier than usual. "Oh, no," she replied, "not a vacation. Thinking about retirement. At least I was..." "Really!" I said. "In Florida?"

Tears unexpectedly sprang up in Paula's eyes. She turned her head away from me quickly, but I heard the emotion in her voice when she spoke. "Yes, well, I'm thinking about it." She turned back to me with a shaky smile. "My friend Trude moved there, to Fisher Island, a few years ago and she loves it. She's been after me for a while to move down."

She reached up and plucked a picture frame off the shelf above the desk. It contained a yellowed newspaper photograph of three people standing in front of a bar, smiling. Based on the hairstyles and fashions on the two women in the picture, I'd guess it had been taken some time in the late '60s. She handed it to me, pointing to the woman on the left. "That's Trude. That was taken at the opening of the very first bar we owned together."

The top line of the caption was visible at the bottom of the frame: (l to r) Partners Trude Heller, Salvatore Piscatelli and Paula Cummings at the successful opening of..." The clipping was cut off there. I'd heard of Trude Heller of course. She'd produced a landmark concert with the Supremes at Lincoln Center in 1965. The iconic Joe Eula poster from that event had hung on my bedroom wall all through my high school years. I didn't recognize the guy standing between the two women. He towered over them, sporting shoulder-length hair and a mustache. "And of course, that's me," she said, indicating the other girl. I stared in shock at the image of young Paula, a stunning brunette in a miniskirt and knee-high boots.

"That's you?" I said, unable to hide the shock in my voice. "Wow! You were hot!" "Well, you don't have to sound so surprised!" Paula snapped, taking the picture back from me."

"Oh, geez, I'm sorry, I, I..." I stammered, "I didn't mean - I mean, you still look – "I struggled to find a word— "fine. You're just different. It took me by surprise..." I trailed off, knowing I wasn't making it any better and should probably just shut up. Paula sat there, looking at me. "I better go see if Diane needs anything else," I mumbled. Turning away from her, I made a fast retreat to the stairs, moving pretty quickly for a guy with both feet in his mouth.

CHAPTER FOUR

Things had cleared out considerably by the time I came back upstairs. There were only about a dozen or so people at the bar and scattered around the room. Diane was down the end of the bar nearest the door, talking to a short heavyset woman wearing a cape, a beret, and a pair of cat's-eye glasses. When she saw me, she waved me over and said, "Billy, this is the friend I wanted you to meet. Samantha, this is Billy, who I told you about. Billy, this is Samantha Bigelow."

I'd heard of Samantha Bigelow. Back in the '70s when I'd first moved to New York, she was a hotshot investigative reporter for the Village Voice. She made her name with a series of articles exposing some kind of government corruption - I don't remember whether it was the police department or City Hall, but suddenly she was the golden child of investigative journalism. Her career exploded, and she seemed to be everywhere. Then sometime in the 80s she had a spectacular fall from grace when it was discovered that she'd falsified facts, quoted sources who later denied their statements, and in one case allegedly created an entirely fictional source for one of her stories. Fired by the Voice, she disappeared in a cloud of humiliation and disgrace.

And now, here she was, sitting at the bar at Characters. "Nice to meet you," I said. "How do you two know each other?" I asked. Diane poured some Jack Daniels over ice, placed the drink in front of me and said, "Through Paula."

"Paula and I lived together a lifetime ago," Samantha said. "Way before she got involved with this one." She smiled at Diane, and I smiled too, not sure what to say to that. I knew Paula and Diane were friends, in fact that was how Diane had gotten her job. I was surprised to hear them referred to as a couple, though. Waddya know? I thought.

Samantha lit a cigarette and turned to me. "So, Diane tells me you might have some good stories for me." "Huh?" I responded eloquently. Diane jumped in. "Samantha writes a column for the West Side News." "'Samantha Bigelow's West Side Stories,' maybe you've read it..." Samantha said. "Um, no, I don't think so. What paper is it in again?" I asked her. "The West Side News."

"Huh. No, I've never read it." Or even heard of it. Samantha looked momentarily miffed but recovered quickly to explain, "That's understandable, we haven't been around long at all. We cover stories related to and about events exclusive to the west side of Manhattan." Well, that sounds ridiculous, I thought. "Is there an East Side News?" I asked.

"What?" Samantha said, clearly thrown by my question. "Well, no," she replied, "at least not yet anyway. But if the West Side News takes off and grows the way it's expected to, I'm sure there will be down the road." Yeah, I was pretty sure that was never gonna happen. "So, what kind of a column do you write?" I asked her.

She made a face and shrugged. "Well right now I'm doing a lot of human interest and celebrity gossip pieces. But that's only until I can get back to the investigative stuff I used to do." She took a big drag on her cigarette and blew out the smoke in a long, slow exhale. "I was just telling Diane that I'm having a rough time with this gossip crap."

"How so?" I asked. "Well for starters, I'm competing with Liz Smith in the Daily News and Cindy Adams in the Post." Liz Smith and Cindy Adams are the current national queens of 'celebrity reporting,' i.e., gossip. They each write daily syndicated newspaper columns that are read by millions. In addition to her popular national column, Liz Smith also appears as a regular on 'Live at Five' here in New York.

"Any publicist worth his paycheck is going to contact one of them if he has an item he wants planted in a column," Samantha continued. "I'm definitely the low woman on that totem pole and that's not going to change. I need to cultivate outside sources. That's why I wanted to meet you." I raised my eyebrows and looked at her. "Me? How do I figure into this?"

Diane leaned in across the bar. "You see a lot of stuff going on here at night. You've told me a few stories that I think are the kind of thing Samantha could use. Like the Ethan Hawke story…" Ethan Hawke? I thought back.

Ethan Hawke had come in with some girl. It was early and the bar was slow. I didn't recognize him. We shot some pool, me and Fat Sara against the two of them. Later, after they'd left, Miguel was talking to Paco, one of the regulars. "Hey Billy," Paco yelled out, "What was the name of the guy you were shooting pool with? The guy from 'Reality Bites' -"

I looked at him. "'Reality Bites?'" And then the penny dropped. "Ohhh—!" I said. "That was Ethan Hawke, wasn't it?" "Ethan Hawke!" Paco said. "That's his name!" He turned to Miguel. "Billy and Fat Sara played them at pool and beat them! Twice!" Miguel laughed and high fived me.

I told Samantha the story, and said, "So you can see, there's no story there, It was just a celebrity sighting. Except I wouldn't even call it that, because nobody recognized him while he was here — well, Paco did, but he didn't tell anybody until after Ethan Hawke had already left."

"Oh, Sweetie, you are so wrong." She attacked the ashtray with her cigarette, extinguishing it with a series of short violent jabs. "It's all the way you spin it. I could've written that up into a great little item. You got anything else, anything recent?" I thought for a minute. "Well," I said, "Erin Murphy was in last night. She played Tabitha on 'Bewitched.'"

"Tabitha was in here? No shit!" She threw her head back and laughed, It wasn't an attractive sound, sort of a raspy bray, like a donkey who smoked two packs a day. "So, spill! What'd she do?" I shrugged. "Nothing. I mean, she hung out for a while, had a couple of drinks, and then left. Again, no story. Sorry."

"Did she see Miguel?" Diane asked. I looked from Diane to Samantha and back at Diane again. "Uhh…What do you mean?" I said. Diane lowered her voice. "Don't worry, it's all right. She knows all about Miguel," she said, indicating Samantha.

"She does?" I said. "'I don't know. I'm not really comfortable talking about Miguel's business…" Samantha, seeing my reticence, jumped in. "Did I mention there'd be a monetary stipend for anything you feed me that I use? It won't be a lot, at least not at first, but that could change." I still hesitated. "It's not about money," I said, "I'm just not sure -"

"Listen, Kid," she said, "I'm not an idiot. And I'm definitely not looking to make any trouble for any of you. I can polish these things up into items that will be absolute gossip gold! I'm that good!" Well, someone's a little full of herself, I thought.

"And" she continued, "I can do it in such a way that everybody's protected, and nobody knows where the stuff comes from." "I need to think about it, " I said. "All right, you think about it while I visit the little girls' room." She looked at Diane. "Do I need a key for the bathroom?"

We kept the key to the ladies' room behind the bar, and Diane handed it to Samantha. I watched her make her way into the bathroom with her cape flapping behind her and then turned to Diane. "What do you think?" I asked her.

"You know what I think, that's why I introduced you. If I could do it for her myself I would, but you know nothing happens here during the day. Unless she wants to write about Old Man Eddie, I've got nothing."

I looked down to the other end of the bar where Old Man Eddie sat nursing a pitcher of beer. The thought of anybody writing about Old Man Eddie made me smile. Eddie was a neighborhood fixture. He'd lost his wife a few years earlier and was all alone now. People told me that before she passed, when she became too weak to continue their daily walks together, he would wheel her around the neighborhood in a shopping cart. Eddie was Diane's one regular. He would show up every day at twelve o'clock when the bar opened and would still be sitting there when the shift changed at 8 o'clock and I came on.

Sometimes he'd hang around for a couple of hours into my shift, especially if I gave him a free pitcher. He liked to shoot pool, and when I first started working there, he taught me the game. He was good, really good, and supposedly had been taught by Minnesota Fats himself. He loved to break my balls when he was teaching me, saying in his gravelly old man voice, "C'mon, get your shit together. We ain't playing tiddlywinks here!"

He nicknamed me 'Tiddlywinks," and delighted in calling me that, thinking it was hilarious. And it was, until I eventually got so good he couldn't beat me anymore. That pissed him off, especially when I'd throw his 'tiddlywinks' line back at him when he lost. But I think he secretly took pride in the fact that it was his tutelage that made my winning possible.

Samantha lumbered back from the bathroom and plopped heavily back onto the bar stool. "So, what do you think?" she asked. I looked at her for a minute, then said, "Yes. Tabitha was here to see Miguel. She spent some time in the bathroom, hung out to have a couple of drinks and left." Samantha smiled broadly. "Thank you. Now that wasn't so hard, was it?" She glanced at her watch, then finished off her drink and stood up. "Can I ask you something?" she said. "What's that?" I said. "Diane and Paula both tell me the crowd here at night is pretty rough. I was just wondering how a little guy like you handles it all alone?"

I let the veiled insult slide and thought a moment. "Well, for starters, there's always regulars around who would have my back if anything happened, so I'm not really alone. I know it looks that way to somebody who just walks in off the street. In fact, I can always tell when someone's thinking exactly what you just asked me."

"So what do you do?" "Nothing," I shrugged. "I don't have to. I leave it to them to figure out. Most of them conclude that nobody's fucking with me because I must be either crazy, connected or carrying. It's the only explanation they can think of. I just let them think it."

"Ha!" Samantha cackled. "I like that! Crazy, connected or carrying! The three C's. I like that!" She rummaged in her purse and pulled out a card and a twenty-dollar bill. "This is my number. Call me anytime, anytime at all. If I don't answer, just leave a message on my machine and I'll get right back to you."

"Roger that!" I said, plucking the card and the bill from her hand. "I like you, kid! I feel good about this!" Adjusting the beret on her head and pulling the cape around her, she looked back and forth between the two of us. "And don't worry, Paula won't know anything about any of this, this is just between the three of us."

She turned and headed toward the door. "Diane, tell Paula I had to run, and I'll touch base with her later. Stay positive, honey, I'll get you to Florida!" What the hell was it with Florida today? Just before exiting, Samantha turned to me. "Pick up a copy of The West Side News tomorrow and check out your first item in print. And listen, make sure you keep in touch. Diane, I'll talk to you later!" she said and sailed out the door.

I turned to Diane. "What did she mean about Florida?" I asked. "I don't know. She's Paula's friend, really, not mine. I don't understand half of what she says to me." All of a sudden she threw her hands in the air. "Shit, she didn't bring back the key!" She walked back to the bathroom door and tried the knob. It was locked. "Oh, hell, she must have locked it inside." "Well, that sucks," I said. "How are we going to get it open?"

Diane came back behind the bar and pulled her purse out of one of the drawers behind the bar. "Not a problem," she said to me, going back to the bathroom. I watched from the bar as she pulled something from her purse. She bent over the doorknob, her back to me, and I could see her arms moving in short jerky motions. After about thirty seconds, she swung the door open. "Voila!" she said. She went into the room and came out holding up the bathroom key. She hung the key back behind the bar on a hook next to the phone.

"How did you do that?" I asked. "Did you just pick the lock?" Diane laughed. "Yeah. Piece of cake, the lock's not that great." "Wow!" I said. "Where the hell did you learn how to do that?" "Legacy from my childhood." she replied. "One of my stepfathers made his living picking pockets, locks and horses. He taught me everything he knows. I can pick anything you put in front of me." "Why don't you pick your nose?" yelled Old Man Eddie from the end of the bar. Just when you think you know someone, I thought.

CHAPTER FIVE

Deep down, I'm a very shallow person. I know that they say, to really know someone you have to scratch the surface; but if you scratch my surface, chances are pretty good you're just going to find more surface.

Even as a little starstruck kid in West Haven, Connecticut, where I grew up, I was extremely superficial, fascinated by stories about show business and its stars. So when I moved to New York City, it was tantamount to Dorothy landing in Oz. I was living in Greenwich Village, long known as the epicenter for artists, actors, activists, writers, and musicians. There were famous faces everywhere!

Walking around my neighborhood, I was like a kid in a candy store. I'd see John Belushi, who was living right around the corner from me at the time, or Richard Gere, who had an apartment two blocks over on Tenth St. I met the construction worker from the Village People in my A&P and Bette Midler in the Blue Mill Tavern. I even had a memorable encounter with Greta Garbo in a vegetable market! My quest to collect celebrity scalps was rivaled only by Lucy Ricardo in Hollywood. Lucky for me, there were no stalker laws back then.

And now my predilection for celebrity sightings was possibly going to pay off. The day following my meeting with Samantha I went out to pick up a copy of the West Side News. As it turned out, the store right around the corner from my house sold it. Who knew?

It wasn't nearly as bad as I thought it would be. It had sections devoted to the different neighborhoods (west of Fifth Avenue, of course), from Battery Park up to the Upper West Side. It covered Battery Park, Soho, the West Village, Chelsea, the Theatre District, and the Upper West Side, with news about businesses, restaurants, bars, clubs, shows and events in each respective area. It also carried stories of interest to the locals living in the various neighborhoods.

I found Samantha's column on page six (coincidence?). Mine was the third item in the column. The first was a paragraph on an upcoming luncheon honoring the developer Donald Trump, who was being hailed as the "comeback king" for his professional resurrection after his latest bankruptcy. This was followed by a blurb about Kathie Lee Gifford being tapped to sing the National Anthem at the upcoming Super Bowl. And then, there it was:

> *"In celebrity news, Erin Murphy, little Tabitha from the beloved television series Bewitched, is in town. Erin might not have grown up to be a practicing witch, but my sources tell me that she still had the magic to make it snow in October here in the West Village! What a Character!!"*

I skimmed the rest of the column. What a piece of crap, I thought. I couldn't believe Samantha, a once respected journalist, was reduced to peddling this kind of tripe. What was she thinking?

Of course, that didn't stop me from enabling her, and over the next few weeks I fed her numerous items about people who'd stopped into Characters. Ben Stiller and Janeane Garofolo sat at the bar one night talking about Stiller's TV show that was rumored to be on track to be cancelled. Another night Ed Harris wandered in by himself and shot pool.

One rainy Tuesday evening Johnny Depp and Mickey Rourke came in with another guy I didn't recognize and a couple of girls. It was early, and the weather was miserable, so the bar was empty. The third guy and one of the girls already appeared to be drunk when they walked in. After getting drinks from me, they all huddled around a table on the back banquette. Standing behind the bar, I could hear the drunk guy's voice, raised and sounding argumentative, while Mickey Rourke talked quietly to him.

After a few minutes, Johnny Depp separated himself from the group and walked to the front of the bar to stand and stare out the window at the rain. I was hoping they'd stay long enough for me to get something for Samantha, but after just a few minutes, Johnny Depp moved toward the door. The others joined him, and they left. I was disappointed but passed the story on anyway. Even Samantha won't be able to make anything out of this, I thought.

Surprisingly, she ran with it. When the incident appeared in Samantha's column the next day, though, she had fleshed it out into something I barely recognized. I'd been noticing, with some alarm, that she'd been taking more and more liberties with the things I was giving her. She was embellishing them outrageously, while still managing to avoid writing anything that could be considered "actionable." By the time they appeared in print, the stories were connected to my original tip by only the thinnest of threads. When I expressed my concern to Samantha, she just laughed it off, told me she knew what she was doing, and raised my pay.

Something more concerning to me, though, were the less and less thinly veiled references she was making about drug use and the bar. None of the celebrities I'd tipped her off about had been there to see Miguel, nor did I ever see anything that made me think they were involved with or doing drugs. Yet in almost every story, Samantha somehow managed to work in a coy innuendo or referral that raised questions and eyebrows. I was beginning to worry about where this could be heading.

CHAPTER SIX

That night at work, Sal, the owner, came in about 8:30. Sal's not a big guy. He's about 5'10" with a wiry build and has a haircut and mustache that make him look like a '70s porn star. But he has a large presence and is extremely personable. People like him.

Sal did time for shooting somebody a few years ago. He told me once that his lawyer was a woman who had been around City Hall for almost forty years and knew where all the bodies were buried; so, despite him being arrested and indicted numerous times over the years, nothing had ever stuck. She'd gotten him off every time. Well, almost every time. Unfortunately for Sal, even her connections couldn't help him when he shot a guy on 14th St. in broad daylight in front of a dozen witnesses. She still got him a sweet deal on sentencing, though, and he was out in less than three years.

He stopped just inside the door to talk to somebody at the pinball machine and then came behind the bar. "What have you got in the register?" he asked me. I indicated the sparse crowd. "Nothing much, yet. Just the bank." He rang up a "No Sale" on the register and the drawer opened. "I'm taking $200," he said. "Stick an IOU in the drawer for me."

He counted out the money and put it in his pocket. I quickly grabbed an envelope from next to the register, scribbled the IOU and held it out to him. "Here," I said. "Do me a favor and sign it so I don't have Mitzi calling me tomorrow."

Mitzi and Sal referred to each other as husband and wife but I don't think they'd ever actually married. They've been together a long time. Mitzi handles the accounting for the bar. When I'd first started working there, Sal would take money from the register a few times a week. One day Mitzi called me at home to ask me about a $100 shortage in the cash drawer from the night before.

"Sal took it," I told her. "What do you mean 'Sal took it'," she asked me. "I mean that Sal came up to me at the bar last night and told me to give him $!00 out of the register." "Son of a bitch!" she shrieked. "And you gave it to him?" "Uhh...yeah. I mean it's his bar, right?" I asked. "It's his money...." "No, it isn't!" she shouted. Huh?

"Listen," she continued. "I waste an entire morning trying to make the register receipts balance against the damn drawer whenever this happens. Don't let him take money out of the register anymore," she said.

I pulled the receiver away from my ear and looked at the phone in disbelief. Does this crazy woman seriously think I can prevent Sal from doing anything he wants to in his own bar? What was she smoking? Putting the phone back against my ear, I smiled and said, "Sure, Mitzi, whatever you say. You got any suggestions for me about how I might do that?"

Of course, my question was met with complete silence. She knew as well as I, that Sal was going to do whatever the hell he wanted to, and nobody, certainly not me, was going to stop him. "Look," I told her. "I have an idea. How about when he does take money, I have him sign an IOU and stick it in the drawer. It won't solve the money shortage problem, but at least you'll know where it went. This way if the drawer comes up short, you'll know why, and can balance your books...."

After huffing and puffing for a few minutes, she finally - reluctantly - agreed to this solution. I knew it didn't sit well with her, but what could she do? I didn't want to say it at the time, but it would also prevent Sal from lying to her and saying he didn't know anything about the missing money. It was something I suspected he'd done in the past, putting the onus on me. Thankfully, Mitzi knew us both well enough to figure it out.

So on this night, after taking the $200, he took the envelope I held out to him and scribbled his name on it before thrusting it back in my hand. "Here. Put it in the damn drawer so I don't have to listen to her either," he said, laughing. Grabbing a beer from the refrigerator, he opened it and headed for the door leading downstairs. "Let me know when Miguel shows up," he said.

Well, that explains the need for the $200, I thought. Despite letting Miguel operate out of his bar, Sal always paid Miguel for anything he got from him. I was surprised when I first realized this. I assumed part of the quid pro quo in their arrangement would be free coke for Sal, but that wasn't the case.

It's not like Sal wasn't benefitting from their arrangement, though. Miguel's presence at Characters guaranteed Sal a full bar every night of the week. And everybody drank. Miguel didn't deal with anyone who would walk into the bar and make a beeline right past me to him. He'd tell them to order something and said he would talk to them after they got a drink. He didn't care that they had a cab waiting, or were double parked, everybody had to spend at the bar. And tip.

Of course, he didn't do this just for the benefit of the bar. We knew that not everybody who came to the bar came to see him. A lot, or at least some of the customers were just that — normal customers. Miguel knew that a stream of people coming into the bar and going right back out again would attract unwanted attention, something we wanted to avoid. Shortly after Sal went downstairs, Sonny Peanuts came in. At 6'3", with his shaved head and tinted glasses, he was easy to spot. He waved at me over the heads of the people at the bar and I pointed downstairs to let him know where Sal was.

Sonny and Sal had grown up together in the neighborhood and had been friends since they were kids. Sal told me that Sonny was like an older brother to him. He said Sonny always looked out for him, and when Sal was sent away Sonny made sure Mitzi was taken care of while he was gone.

Sonny Peanuts was rumored to be a made man. He got his name because in addition to the jukebox, Sonny also holds the concession on the peanut dispensers, not just in Characters but in bars all over the city. The peanut dispenser looks like an old gumball machine. It stands between the pinball machine and the jukebox against the wall across from the bar. I can't imagine what kind of income a peanut dispenser generates, but it must add up, especially when you multiply it by the number of machines he runs.

The jukebox, on the other hand, is a gold mine. Sonny comes in once or twice a week and, with the use of a special key, removes a long drawer set vertically into the side of the machine. I watched now as he pulled the drawer out and emptied it, marveling again at the eye-popping amount of bills it held. Removing the bills from the tray, he separated them into small, folded stacks before transferring them to the pockets of his pants, jacket, and shirt

When he was done, he replaced the drawer in its slot at the bottom of the jukebox. Standing up, he shook out his pants, brushed off his hands, and cast another look around the room. After throwing another nod my way, he opened the door to the basement and disappeared downstairs. What a character, I thought as I stood watching him. It occurred to me, not for the first time, just how serendipitous the name Sal had chosen for his bar really was.

CHAPTER SEVEN

The day after the Johnny Depp item ran in Samantha's column, Jeremy called me from South Carolina to check in. He was shooting a TV-movie called 'Twisted Desire' with Daniel Baldwin and the girl who played Sabrina, the Teenage Witch. "So, how's it going down there?" I asked him. "I really miss New York," he said. "I can't wait to get back. It's so boring here."

Jeremy is only twenty-two years old. He'd already had a successful career as a pop singer by the time I met him, though to be honest, I'd never heard of him. He wandered into the bar by chance one night and we hit it off, quickly becoming friends. He had just moved to New York from LA and was trying to transition his career from singing to acting. He was doing well and had been getting a lot of work that required him to travel out of town. Because of this, he'd yet to get a place of his own and had been sleeping on the couch at his agent's apartment when he was in the city. Within a few days of meeting each other, he had moved into my place.

"Have you gone out down there at all?" I asked him. "Not really. There hasn't been anybody to hang out with. The crew is all really old." "Waddya mean?" I asked him. "How old?" "I don't know," he said. "they're like in their late '30s and 40s." Ouch! Jeremy forgets I'm twice his age. "What about Daniel Baldwin?" I said.

"Well, Daniel Baldwin's wife Elizabeth flew down here with him two weeks ago, so they were spending all their free time with each other. But she flew home yesterday, and check this out: as soon as she was gone, he asked me if I wanted to go out for drinks with him after dinner last night."

"Wow, that's great," I said. "Where did you go?" "No, that's the thing, it wasn't great. All he really wanted was a wing man to go whoring around with." "What? A wing man?"

"Yeah, I couldn't believe it! For the last two weeks he's been acting like this devoted, loving husband, but as soon as Elizabeth leaves he turns into this total dog." "Oh, man, that sucks," I said.

"Yeah, really." Jeremy sighed. "I ended up leaving him at the last strip club he dragged me to and had to take a cab back to the hotel. And get this: He just asked me if I wanted to go out again tonight…" "Are you gonna go?" I asked. "After last night? No way! Once was bad enough." "Is there anybody else there you can hang out with? What about Sabrina? Melissa what's-her-name?"

"Melissa Joan Hart." He laughed. "That's not gonna happen. I don't think she likes me. She accused me of having alcohol on my breath the other day and got really pissy." "What, you mean while you were filming?" "Yeah, I had to kiss her." "Why would she say that?" I asked him. "Did you?"

"Have alcohol on my breath? Well yeah, maybe, but that's not my point," he said. "She's kind of a bitch. Really uptight. And she's down here with her mother, who's an even bigger bitch than she is, if that's possible." I laughed. "What's going on up there?" he asked. "God, I really miss New York and everybody at the bar. How's Miguel?"

"Miguel? He's the same. You know, business as usual." Jeremy persisted. "C'mon, Billy, there's nothing new? I'm dying down here I'm so bored. Tell me something -" "I know what I can tell you about," I said, and then related the story of Samantha and my recent involvement with her. "That's so funny," he said when I finished. "And this lady Samantha just prints anything you tell her?"

"So far, yes. It's insane! She not only prints it, but she embellishes it like you wouldn't believe! I guess it's helping her get whatever it is she's trying to accomplish, though. She told me last week that her column is starting to get some buzz from 'the right people,' whoever they are. And she was real wound up about being contacted by somebody she used to work with at the Village Voice, something about something that could lead to something –"

"That's a lot of 'somethings'," Jeremy said. I laughed. "Yeah, I know.... She's calling me at the bar almost every night, bugging me. I'm starting to feel a little uncomfortable with her…"

"Why is that?" he asked. I thought for a minute before answering him. "I don't know. I guess mostly I'm worried that she's going to attract the attention of the wrong people. How many times can you allude to coke in reference to a bar in the West Village and call someone a 'Character' with a capital 'C' before someone puts two and two together?"

"Yeah, I see what you mean," he said. "Especially with them raiding all those small bars everywhere. Is that still happening?"

"Oh yeah!" I told him. "Another bar over on Avenue B got raided last week." Since Rudy Giuliani has become mayor of New York, he's been making a big show about dealing with 'the drug scourge.' His office is working with the DEA in a highly publicized campaign to crack down on neighborhood bars and places known for drug trafficking, like Washington Square Park.

"What's Miguel think about all of this?" Jeremy asked me. "Miguel?" I asked, surprised. I hadn't given any thought to how Miguel might react if he got wind of Samantha's columns. "As far as I know, he doesn't know anything about it. Not yet, anyway. I sure as hell haven't said anything to him. Hopefully he'll stay in the dark until I can figure out how to handle this."

"Well, that's easy," Jeremy said. "Just stop telling her stuff." Ah, the wisdom of youth. He was right, of course, and I knew it. I also knew that I was enjoying not only the extra income I was bringing in, but also the jolt of excitement I got from seeing stories in print that I'd had a hand in creating.

"I thought of that," I told him, "Or, I was thinking of maybe trying to give her stuff that has no connection to the bar. Get her on a different track, maybe." We were both quiet for a moment, mulling this over, when Jeremy suddenly piped up, "Give her my Daniel Baldwin story." "What? Dude, that would be awesome," I laughed, then stopped and thought about it. "No, I can't do that," I told him. "What if it got traced back to you as the source?"

"How would it get traced back to me?" he said. "You said yourself, nobody reads this paper. He'll probably never even hear about it, right?" "But won't you feel guilty? It's kind of a shitty thing to tell people about. He's going to come off like a real jerk."

Jeremy cackled, "That's great, he is a real jerk! Listen, his wife was really sweet when she was here, I liked her a lot. And he's a freaking pig, so no, I wouldn't feel bad at all if people found out."

I ran it over in my head. I knew it was the kind of story Samantha would love and it wasn't connected to the bar in any way, which was great. At the very least, it might get her off my back for a while. And, I thought with a smile, the chance of Daniel Baldwin ever seeing a copy of the West Side News, especially since he was in South Carolina, was virtually non-existent.

"What was the name of the strip club you went to?" I asked him. "Jeez, which one? I think we hit every single one in the city. You got a pen?" I did, and for the next ten minutes Jeremy gave me every sordid detail of his night out on the town with Daniel Baldwin. Just before he hung up he said, "Hey, feel free to tell Samantha that Melissa Joan Hart is a real bitch, too!" I could hear him laughing as I hung up the phone.

CHAPTER EIGHT

The bar was quiet when I got to work that night. Thursdays always start slow. A lot of people stay in to watch "Friends" and "Seinfeld", so things generally don't start to pick up until 10 o'clock or so. As the night went on, it shaped up in a typical fashion. Some friends from Roebling's, the restaurant I'd worked at prior to Characters stopped in, but didn't stay long. The usual regulars all trickled in at some point, including one of my favorite people, Fat Sara.

Fat Sara's in love with Sal. They've been having an affair since long before I knew either one of them. A nightly regular, when Sal isn't around she keeps a proprietary eye on everything and reports back to him. She also plays a critical role in keeping the bar off the radar.

In New York City, any disturbance at a bar that requires police involvement is reported to the state liquor commission. If a bar gets cited enough times, renewal of its license can be imperiled. That fact, and knowing what closer scrutiny of Characters might reveal, makes it essential to avoid any attention from the state and local authorities.

Fat Sara works around the corner from Characters at St. Vincent's Hospital, where she mans the admissions desk in the emergency room from four until midnight. If there's a fight in the bar that results in a customer needing medical attention, we send them right over to Sara at the St. Vincent's emergency room. Once there, she uses her considerable powers of persuasion to make sure the victim doesn't notify the police. If they're adamant about reporting it, she manages to convince them it would be in their best interest to tell the police the attack occurred on the street or getting off the subway and deflect attention away from the bar. Consequently, in all the years I've been at Characters, the police have never been called to investigate an incident complaint.

Another favorite regular, Black Lil, showed up a little before twelve. Black Lil lives right across the river in Jersey City and is supposed to have lived with Miles Davis back in the '60s. Now she works the third shift at the phone company right around the corner on 14th St., which allows her to get to the bar by midnight most nights. Back before I started working there, Black Lil and Fat Sara were the only two women who used to hang out at Characters. Like Paula, the bar's reputation scared a lot of women away. I've managed to turn that around over the course of the last year, and most nights now there's a pretty even mix of men and women. No matter what, though, I can still count on Black Lil and Fat Sara to put in their nightly appearances.

Lil took a seat at the bar next to two other customers I was talking to: Deb, a blonde stripper who works at the Doll's House, a gentlemen's club on Murray St. in the financial district, and Deb's mother, Dolly. Dolly accompanies her daughter everywhere, acting as a sort of bodyguard/manager. "Let me have a beer, Darlin'," Lil said to me.

As I opened the cooler to retrieve the beer, she turned to Deb and Dolly. "How are you ladies doing tonight?" she asked the women. "We're great, Lil!" Deb exclaimed, smiling. She looked at her mother, who bobbed her head in excitement. Deb is a bright, pretty girl with a bubbly personality and the biggest set of gravity-defying breasts I've ever seen. She's known professionally as "Mounds Vesuvius" and is touted for her "Twin Volcanoes, the Eighth Natural Wonder of the World."

I know it's a well-worn cliché that a lot of strippers only strip as a way to put themselves through college, but Deb is the real deal. She has her undergrad degree, is currently taking graduate courses, and has already been accepted to Medical School. Guided by Mama's shrewd management, the stripping is merely the means to pay for that end.

"We're better than great," Dolly proclaimed, reaching for the oversize purse she always carries with her. Dolly might have been pretty once; but her once zaftig figure has now gone to fat, and her hair is thin and wiry from a lifetime of being subjected to punishing dyes and bleaches.

My mother used to tell my brother and me that girls turn into their mothers. "If you want to know what a girl's going to look like when she's older," she'd say, "just look at her mother." Seeing Deb and Dolly sitting side by side, I had the unkind thought that, if my mother was right, it was probably a good thing Deb would be moving on to a career where physical appearance wouldn't matter.

Pulling her purse over in front of her, Dolly looked around to make sure nobody was paying attention to us. Apparently satisfied, she opened up the bag so Lil and I could see its contents. "Look at this," she said, reaching inside. Without pulling it out, she showed us a roll of bills held together by a rubber band. She rotated it inside the bag so we could see the heft of the bankroll, which looked to be about four inches thick and comprised of ten-dollar bills.

"Damn, girl," Lil said, looking at Deb. Turning her head to me as I put her beer down on the bar, she said, "We're in the wrong line of work, Billy." "No shit!" I said, laughing. I looked at Deb. "You made that tonight?" I asked. Deb and her mother exchanged glances. "We started a new side-line," Deb told us. "It was Mama's idea, and we weren't really sure it was going to work, but we started tonight and it was great," she said, her eyes sparkling.

Lil caught my eye and raised her eyebrows. Looking at Dolly, she asked, "What kind of a side-line are you running, Dolly? Is it legal?" "Completely," Dolly replied, laughing. "And so simple, I'm kicking myself for not thinking of it years ago." She paused, then blurted, "We're selling photos." "Selling photos?" I asked. "You mean, like 8 X 10 publicity shots of Mounds Vesuvius?"

Dolly, shaking her head, began to dig in her purse. She pulled out various items and set them aside on the bar as she rummaged around, making a small pile in the process of pasties, a G-string, tubes of glitter, a feather boa, a fan, and even a pair of shoes. I was waiting for a wall mirror, potted plant, and coat rack to emerge. Eventually, she found what she'd been looking for and pulled out a Polaroid camera, setting it down on the bar.

I looked at the camera. "You sell Polaroid photos?" I asked. I turned to Deb. "Of you?" "And my fans," she said. I waited, still not understanding. "After Debbie finishes her set downstairs at the bar," Dolly explained, "we announce that fans can have individual pictures taken with Mounds Vesuvius for ten dollars each. There's a room upstairs they let us use. The guys line up on the staircase. One at a time, I walk them into the room and over to a small platform, where they stand with Deb."

Lil opened her mouth to say something, but Dolly cut her off. "They're not allowed to touch her, "she said, anticipating Lil's question. "But sometimes I'll take their arm or put my arm around their shoulders for the photo," Deb offered. Dolly continued. "I take the picture, they give me ten bucks, and I bring in the next one. It takes about fifteen seconds for each guy." She took a sip from her glass. "We sold over two hundred pictures tonight."

"Two hundred pictures?" I asked. "In less than an hour," she answered. "And that was after just one show. On weekends, she does three sets, and we'll do a photo shoot after each one." My jaw dropped. Two hundred pictures at ten dollars a pop, earned in less than an hour! I calculated the amount of money their new venture was going to make them (over and above Deb's regular salary and tips) and stared in open-mouthed astonishment. And it was all cash. Damn, I wish I had tits!

As we were talking, I saw Australian Kenny walk into the bar and wander to the back of the room. Kenny is a fairly new regular, having just arrived in New York from his native Australia last month. He'd come to the city as part of a touring dance company. He liked the city so much, he told me, that when they returned home he decided to defect, quit his dance troupe, and stay in New York. I didn't point out to him that technically I don't think you can defect from Australia.

Kenny says he was born a hermaphrodite and claims to have two sets of genitalia - male and female. When he runs out of money, which is frequently, he offers to show his genitalia to people in exchange for the price of a drink. He gets a surprising number of positive responses to this offer. Of course, I always make them go into the bathroom for the reveal.

A little after one, Buzzy showed up wearing a tuxedo, having come from some black-tie event in midtown. Buzzy is old, black, and gay. A true gentleman, he's quiet and soft spoken, and teaches history at Columbia University. He also has a great sense of humor. I once heard him say, "I'm so old, I lent Jesus money!" The next time I heard him reference his age, I said to him, "Honey, you're so old, you blew Jesus!" He loved it.

The first and only rule Sal laid down for me when I first started working for him was that Buzzy had carte blanche. He was never to pay for anything. Ever. I found out later that Sal had been acquitted on an attempted murder charge, thanks to Buzzy. This respectable college professor, who had no obvious connection to the defendant, had taken the stand at Sal's trial and swore he was with him at the time of the crime. In short, Buzzy perjured himself. The jury believed him, and Sal was acquitted. Sal got off, and Buzzy got free drinks for life.

I walked over to Lil, who was now sitting alone. "What happened to Deb and Dolly?" I asked her as she turned to wave Buzzy over. "They went home to count their money," Lil answered. "I hope to hell Dolly carries a gun in that Mary Poppins purse of hers if she's gonna walk around with that kind of cash."

I laughed at her "Mary Poppins" reference, having had the same thought myself. I threw a napkin down on the bar as Buzzy slid into the seat beside her. "Don't you look nice!" Lil exclaimed, eyeing his tuxedo. "Why thank you, Dear," Buzzy replied. "And you look lovely, as usual." Lil snorted. "Oh, please! Billy...!" she said, "Get Buzzy a drink!" "Already done," I said as I placed a vodka martini in front of him. Lil pulled a bill from the change she had sitting on the bar in front of her and handed it to me. "Here," she said, "take it out of this."

As I turned to the register, I heard Buzzy say in his soft, cultured voice, "Why, thank you, Lillian. But don't think you're going to get into my pants tonight," followed by Lil's guffaw as she slapped the bar. Smiling, I rang up the sale, gave Lil her change and surveyed the room. It was a good crowd tonight. I was enjoying it, and everything was running smoothly. Then at 1:30, the door opened, and trouble walked in.

CHAPTER NINE

I had dealt with this girl in the past. In fact, I had thrown her out of the bar just the week before. She'd gotten the key to the ladies' room that night, went in, locked the door and passed out. It took nearly half an hour of pounding on the door before she roused herself enough to unlock it. I escorted her out and told her in no uncertain terms that she was eighty-sixed and not to come back.

And now, here she was. I came out from behind the bar and met her just inside the door. "You can't come in," I told her. "You've been eighty-sixed." "I know, I know, but PLEASE, won't you let me use the bathroom? I really really need to use the bathroom. PLEASE!" I looked at her closely. Even in the dim bar light I could see she was deathly pale and had a slight sheen of sweat on her face. She was twitching and shaking and looked to be on the verge of tears.

"Please, please," she said. "I have to pee so bad! I'll be fast, I promise, and then I'll leave. There's nowhere else around here with a bathroom! Please!" Against my better judgement I relented. "All right," I said, "but I'm not giving you the key. I'll unlock the door for you and give you five minutes. If you're not out of there in five minutes, I'll come in and drag you out. Don't make me do that."

"I won't, I promise!" she said and headed toward the bathroom. "Hurry, please!" she cried over her shoulder. I grabbed the key, unlocked the door, and stepped aside. She rushed past me and pushed the door shut behind her. I heard her throw the lock and walked back to the bar, holding the key. Miguel strolled over to the end of the bar where I was standing in front of Buzzy and Lil. "Billy, that girl's bad news," he said to me softly.

"Yeah, I know but I didn't want to be a total dick. She'll be gone in five minutes. Do you know her?" I asked him. "No, not me. She's not interested in what I have." Black Lil chimed in. "Uh-huh. you got that right." I looked back and forth between them. "What are you talking about?" I asked. Miguel looked at me. "That girl's a junkie. You shouldn't let her in here. She's probably using the bathroom right now to shoot up…"

Before I could reply, the bathroom door began shaking with a loud banging. It sounded like something was being hit against the inside of the door with a steady repetitive pounding. We all turned toward the sound. "What the fuck is that?" I said. We all froze and listened to the thumping. Suddenly Black Lil got up off her barstool so quickly she knocked over her drink. "Oh my God!" she cried. "Billy, get the key! She's convulsing!'

I grabbed the key, and we ran to the bathroom. I unlocked the door and tried to push it open but couldn't. Something was blocking it on the other side. With Miguel's help I was able to open it enough to see it was the girl's body. She was sprawled on the floor with the upper half of her body against the door. There was a needle still hanging precariously out of her left arm. Her eyes were rolled up in her head and she continued to convulse and bounce against the door. Black Lil leaned over me to look in.

"She's OD'ing," she stated matter-of-factly. She turned around and faced the bar. "Does anybody have saline solution?" she called out. "C'mon, who wears contacts? I need saline solution NOW!"

Brania Feldstein, another regular, yelled out, "I have some!" She pulled her purse off the back of her barstool and rushed toward us, pulling the bottle out of her purse and handing it to Lil. Lil pushed me to the side and squeezed through the opening into the bathroom. As I stood watching, Black Lil carefully removed the hypodermic from the still convulsing girl's arm. She stuck the needle in the bottle of saline solution and using the plunger, filled it and injected its contents into the girl's arm. I watched frozen, not knowing what to expect.

Lil took the bar rag I'd been holding and held it under the faucet. She took the damp cloth and started to wipe the girl's face, and as we watched, the girl slowly stopped convulsing and shaking. Her color gradually returned to her face, and she started to breathe regularly. Lil leaned into her and was murmuring something in her ear.

I looked around and caught Brania's eye. "Go hail a cab out in front," I told her. "We'll be right out." I watched as she walked through the bar and exited out the front door before turning my attention back to the bathroom. Lil was still kneeling on the floor talking to the girl. She looked at me. "I found out where she lives. Help me get her up."

Miguel and Paco went into action and together got the girl on her feet. Supporting her as they walked her out the front door, Black Lil walked next to her, keeping up a constant low murmur of conversation. I watched through the front window as they helped her into the back seat of the waiting cab then saw Lil slip a bill to the cab driver and speak to him briefly. The cab drove off and Miguel, Paco, Lil and Brania reentered, crossed to the bar and sat down.

I handed Lil two twenties out of my tip cup. "What did you give the cabby? Is this enough?" Lil waved it away. "That's too much, Darlin'." "Just take it," I said. "You just saved that girl's life, There's no way you should pay for her cab home, too!" "Okay, " she replied, taking the money. "Thank you."

"No, thank you!" I said. I set rocks glasses up on the bar and poured huge shots into them. I passed them around and everyone threw back their shot. We looked at each other, nobody knowing quite what to say. Then we all started laughing. "What the hell just happened?" Brania asked. "What the fuck was that?!?" Lil handed the bottle of saline solution back to Brania. "Here, Honey," she said. "This is yours."

"Eww, I don't want that back, throw it out!" Brania squealed. "You stuck a junkie's needle into that. Do you really think I'd use that in my eyes now?" We were laughing hard now, but there was a slightly manic edge to it. The incident had shaken us all up more than we wanted to admit, and the laughter was a good release.

"Damn, Lil!" I said. "Did that just happen? Did I just watch you pull somebody out of a heroin overdose by injecting them with saline solution? Where the fuck did you learn how to do that?" Lil smiled. "You forget, Darlin'. I lived with Miles Davis."

CHAPTER TEN

I had the next day off and ended up not leaving the house. It was a blustery, wet day, perfect for sleeping late, ordering from Joe Jr's. and camping out under a blanket in front of the television. After the excitement of the night before, I'd completely forgotten about the Daniel Baldwin story I'd passed on to Samantha and hadn't bothered to go out to buy the day's edition of the West Side News.

So it came as a complete shock to me when I turned on Live at Five and saw Liz Smith reporting my Daniel Baldwin story on the air. Well, Samantha's Daniel Baldwin story. At least, I was pretty sure it was. The details Liz Smith was reporting matched each and every detail I'd dictated to Samantha yesterday. I thought it improbable that she'd gotten the story from another source. It was identical to what I'd gotten from Jeremy.

I picked up the phone and called Samantha. She answered on the first ring. "Hello!" she barked. "Who's this?" "Samantha, it's me," I said. "Are you watching Live at Five?" "You bet your ass I am!" she crowed. "Isn't this something? You really struck gold on this one, Kid! Liz Smith is following it up in her column, and I just got word that Page Six is running it as their lead story tomorrow in the Post. This is beyond fabulous!"

"I don't understand," I yelled at her. "How did this happen? How did Liz Smith get this?" "She got it from my column this morning, where the hell do you think she got it?" She paused, and I could hear the click of a lighter in my ear. As I listened, I heard her take a drag on a cigarette and exhale. "What's your problem?" she asked. "This is good for you, too. I'm giving you a bonus." "I don't care about a bonus!" I shouted. "Well, you're getting one anyway. You earned it. Listen, I can't talk right now, I've got too much going on. Call me later," she said, and hung up.

I stood there with the phone in my hand listening to the sudden sound of a dial tone. "Aarrgh!" I growled and slammed the receiver down. I wanted to call Jeremy and give him a head's up, but I had no idea how to reach him. I knew that Live at Five was a local newscast, but I was pretty sure it would only be a matter of time before somebody contacted Daniel Baldwin and told him about it. Even if he didn't hear about it tonight, once it appeared in Liz Smith's column and on Page Six in the morning it was going to be game over. All I could do now is pray that nobody put it together and zeroed in on Jeremy as the source of the story. I was just going to have to wait to hear from him.

I didn't have to wait long. Two hours later he called. "Wow, you wouldn't believe what's going on down here!" he said. "Everything's gone crazy!" "So, I'm assuming Daniel Baldwin heard about the Liz Smith broadcast?" I asked.

"Oh, he heard about it, all right. He's been on the phone for the past hour - his agent, who I think is the one who told him, his wife, the producers, the publicity guy for the movie, his lawyer, everybody! He's out for blood, Billy. He's wants to know where it came from and he's telling them all to find out where she got the story." "Oh, shit, man. Shit shit shit! I am so sorry, J. Do you think they have any idea where it came from?"

"Right now, they're thinking it might be from some local reporter. I guess after I left him that night, Daniel got into it at the strip club with some guy who works for a newspaper down here. I'm not worried, dude. I'm discovering that he's not very well liked by either the production team or the crew. Hell, he's even managed to make some enemies among the locals. Right now, they're thinking this could have come from anybody."

I felt a little of the tension leave my body. "Well, that's good, I suppose...

"Yeah, don't worry about it," he said. "I'm not. Not yet anyway. Let's see what develops, but right now I think we're safe." "Okay, kid" I sighed. "I hope you're right."

CHAPTER ELEVEN

The rain that had been falling on and off all day finally stopped about 11 o'clock that night. Having slept most of the day, I was feeling restless, so after watching Letterman's monologue I decided to go down and see what was going on at the bar.

I walked into Characters, and the first person I saw was Cathy O'Malley. Cathy's sister Irene is married to Danny Pope. Cathy lives with Frankie One-Ball, who got his nickname after an unfortunate encounter with a subway train resulted in him losing a testicle. Frankie was sitting at the bar talking to Cormac, the tough Irish bartender who worked the nights I was off. Cathy was standing by the jukebox, picking selections, and holding a small dog.

"Hey," I said, "where'd ya find the pig?" "Billy, you idiot," she replied. "It's not a pig, it's a dog!" "I was talkin' to the dog," I shot back. Cathy let out an explosive laugh. "You're such an asshole!" she said. "Never said I wasn't," I answered, laughing with her.

Cathy is only 5'4" and weighs about 190. She's funny and has a big heart, and I always have a good time when she and Frankie are around. Danny's wife, Irene is also somebody I like a lot.

There's a third O'Malley sister, Janet. I don't have a lot of good things to say about Janet, so I won't say anything.

"You want a bump?" Cathy asked me. She held out her hand toward me and I could see the familiar packaging of Miguel's product peeking out of her fist. "Oh, no thanks. I'm gonna try and make it an early night." I told her. "Good luck with that, sweetie. Let me know if you change your mind." she responded, and then went back to playing the jukebox.

I headed toward the back of the room. On the way, I stopped at the bar long enough to say 'Hi' to Frankie One-Ball and pick up the Jack on the rocks that Cormac had poured for me when he saw me come in. I thanked him and walked over to the banquette where my friend Edgar was sitting with his girlfriend Amber. I slid into the booth next to them.

"Hey, guys," I said. "What's up?" "Hey, Billy," Edgar said. "Where are you coming from?" "Nowhere, just home," I answered. "This is the first time I've been out all day. Have you two been here all night?" I asked. "I just got here," Amber said. "I don't know how long he's been here!" From her tone I realized I'd walked into the middle of an argument. It seemed like every time I saw them together lately they were in the middle of an argument.

Edgar and Amber are both in their mid-twenties. He works as a DJ, mainly at after-hours clubs, and is starting to enjoy some degree of success. Amber is a 'dancer', the kind of dancer they used to call strippers. She works at a few different places around town. They've been a couple for about three months. "I'm working tonight at a pick-up after-hours place on 37th St.," Edgar told me. "You should come by."

Amber turned to me. "Oh, yes, Billy, come and dance with me." Amber hates going to Edgar's gigs because he likes her to sit with him at the DJ station. He doesn't like her talking and hanging out with other guys and I can't blame him. Amber is tall, blonde, and built. Edgar is short, my height, and not exactly a GQ model. Unfortunately, he knows she's out of his league physically and it makes him insecure and possessive. I like him a lot, so I can't help feeling sorry for him. I think it's a pretty safe bet the relationship is on borrowed time.

"Yeah, Billy, come and hang with Amber." Edgar said. "I'll put you on the list." I knew he was thinking that if I kept Amber occupied, he could relax and do his job without worrying about her. Since I'd slept most of the day and figured I'd be up late anyway, I said, "Sure, I'll come and check it out." So much for having an early night. I left Edgar and Amber and went to find Miguel.

CHAPTER TWELVE

The after-hours place where I was to meet Edgar and Amber was on 37th St. A non-descript commercial four-story brick building, it sat halfway down the block between 8th and 9th Avenues. After entering through a glass door, I passed through a small alcove and went through a second door. Once inside, I encountered two enormous gentlemen, one white and one black, both dressed in tee shirts, leather, denim, and chains.

They each stood well over six feet tall, and together probably added up to a quarter ton of solid muscle. The black guy, who was collecting money, was sitting on a metal chair just inside the door. He had it tilted back against the wall with the front legs off the ground and was rocking up and down. I wondered how long the chair would withstand the punishment before the inevitable occurred.

I gave chair-man my name. Edgar must have added it to the list because after checking the clipboard he gave his buddy a nod. The second guy told me to raise my arms and spread my feet and gave me a thorough pat down. He had huge hands, rough and calloused, which he ran quickly but efficiently all over my body and between my legs. I kind of enjoyed it. When he finished, I thanked him and asked if I could go again. A smile briefly broke his steely facade. He swatted at me and said, "Get the fuck outta here."

I followed a staircase up three flights. At the top of the third flight the stairway opened to a large landing. There were at least four more guys who looked like security lingering at the top of the stairs and just inside the open doorway leading into the 'club.' The room I entered was an enormous loft-like space. To the right, a wall of large windows across the front looked down on 37th St. Two pool tables with red felt sat in front of the windows.

I saw more than a few familiar faces, mostly bartenders and others in the service industry who I knew from their visits to Characters. I returned a couple of waves and a nod and looked around. I turned left and headed toward the back of the room. I passed the bathrooms on the left and the bar on the right before coming to the entrance into a back room where the DJ was set up.

The room had no windows and was painted completely black: Black walls, black floor, and black ceiling. There were multi-level benches built in along three of the walls which were also painted black. The only lighting came from UV black lights positioned to illuminate huge swaths of Day-Glo paint splashed around the walls. I could make out the writhing bodies dancing in the center of the room, silhouetted against the Day-Glo splashes. As my eyes adjusted, I could also see people on the benches smoking cigarettes and weed and taking advantage of the darkness to openly snort out of their cocaine vials. In the most shadowed corners, I spotted more writhing bodies that I don't think were dancing.

Looking across the room I saw Edgar standing on the raised platform against the far wall. He was behind a long table that held the turntables and was holding a set of headphones to his ear with one hand. Amber was seated behind him, somehow looking annoyed and bored at the same time. I crossed the dance floor and made my way over to them.

When I reached the stage I yelled over the music, "Hey, guys!" and waved at them. Edgar waved back with his free hand, and Amber jumped out of her chair. "Oh, Billy, you made it! Yay!" She climbed down off the DJ platform and grabbed my hand. "You don't have a drink yet. C'mon, let's go to the bar." She turned to Edgar. "We're going to the bar. Do you want something?"

Edgar shook his head, holding up a liter bottle of water he was drinking from. He leaned over across the table and shouted in my ear, "Tell them to put it on my tab. And keep an eye on her, okay?" I looked over my shoulder to see if Amber heard him, but she was already halfway across the dance floor on her way to the bar. "Yeah, dude, don't worry," I yelled back. "I'll keep her occupied." I turned and made my way out of the darkness.

CHAPTER THIRTEEN

Amber was already standing at the bar talking to the bartender when I re-entered the front room. I sidled up to her and said, "What are you drinking?" "I already ordered," she said. "What are you having?" I looked at the bartender and said, "Could I get a Jack on the rocks, please?" He went to make our drinks and Amber leaned into me. "Do you have anything on you?" she asked. "Edgar's holding our stuff and I didn't want to ask him to pass it to me in front of everybody."

Like anyone here would care, I thought. I suspected that Edgar was playing some kind of power game, trying to control Amber by controlling the coke. I knew that if he kept acting like this their romance was guaranteed to tank. I handed her my package and watched her go into the Ladies' Room as the bartender returned and placed our drinks in front of me. "I put these on Edgar's tab," he said.

"Thanks," I replied. I threw some bills on the bar for a tip and took a long pull on the Jack Daniels. I started talking to the bartender, whose name turned out to be Brad, and before I knew it my glass was empty and I realized Amber hadn't returned from the bathroom. I signaled to Brad for another and turned to look around for Amber. I finally spotted her across the room talking to somebody I knew slightly.

Ronaldo Sagarro has worked at City Hall for as long as I've known him. I don't know what it is exactly that he does there, but I've seen him on television standing behind the mayor with a bunch of staffers during news conferences. Years ago, before he began working in politics, he had been a male model. He made a lot of money as the face of Salem cigarettes in an international ad campaign targeting Hispanic countries and local communities. He became known as the "Spanish Salem Guy," before giving it up to work in city government.

I hadn't seen him in a while. He'd grown a mustache since the last time I saw him, and while he still had his model good looks, I thought the mustache aged him. Ronaldo lives in a building that rents efficiency apartments right up the block from me on 12th St., and I see him frequently at Joe Jr's. The first time I ever spoke to him was back in the 70's when I was waiting tables at the Riviera Cafe in Sheridan Square. It was summer, and he was sitting by himself in my section. He had on a pair of shorts and was sitting with his right ankle resting on his left knee. His shorts were baggy enough to allow anybody who walked by to see he wasn't wearing underwear. When I dropped the food at his table I leaned over and whispered, "You shouldn't sit like that. Your balls are hanging out."

Incredibly embarrassed, but extremely grateful, he quickly uncrossed his legs and thanked me. Thus began a casual acquaintance that's gone on almost twenty years. Amber finished her conversation with him and came back to the bar. "Sorry," she said. "I got sidelined by some creep." She slipped the coke into my hand, and I slid it back into my pocket. "Are you talking about Ronaldo?" I asked her. "Who?" she said. "Ronaldo. The guy I just saw you talking to."

"Is that his name? I didn't know." She picked up her drink and drained half of it. "He just started talking to me when I came out of the Ladies' Room and I thought he was kind of hot, so I stopped to talk. Then I asked him if he wanted a bump, and he starts freaking lecturing me about he never touches that stuff, it's poison, blah blah blah…What the hell is somebody who doesn't do blow doing in an afterhours club at 4:30 in the morning?"

I wondered the same thing. I remembered from waiting on him at the Riv that he doesn't drink alcohol either. Speaking of which…."What are you drinking?" I asked her. "I asked for a dirty martini," she said, taking another swig. "But it's an after-hours club, so of course they don't have olives." She rolled her eyes and shook her head as if to say, "Can you believe it?" I guess working in the high-class establishments where she takes her clothes off for money in front of strangers has gotten her used to the finer things in life.

"So," I said. "It's a dirty martini without the olive juice and without the olives?" "Yeah, and no vermouth either, 'cuz I don't like it." "So you're drinking a glass of straight vodka-" She emptied the glass in a final gulp and slammed it back on the bar. "And you're drinking a glass of straight whiskey, so what's the problem? Jesus, you sound just like Edgar!"

I laughed and said, "Whoa, back off, girl! I wasn't passing judgement; I was just making conversation. I'm in no position to judge anybody!" She sighed. "I'm sorry. I know you didn't mean anything by it. Edgar's just got me wound so fucking tight — he's starting to drive me crazy. I can't even take a shit lately without him knocking on the bathroom door asking me if I'm okay or do I need anything."

Not really wanting to get into this with her, I said, "He just loves you, Am." "Yeah, well he 'loves' me too much," she replied bitterly. While I was trying to think of a way to change the direction of the conversation, I heard a commotion near the front door. I turned just in time to see a tsunami of blue uniforms pour through the entryway into the room. Suddenly all hell broke loose. "Everybody stay where you are," commanded a voice. "Kill that music and get these lights up!" It was a raid. Well, this is just great, I thought.

The man who seemed to be in charge continued snapping out orders as the armada of cops spread out throughout the club. The music had been cut off and the lights turned on in both the front and back rooms, and now the police were yelling at us to move to the sides of the room and place our hands on the wall. I looked over my shoulder and saw Ronaldo standing near the front entrance talking to the detective who seemed to be in charge, in what appeared to be an intense conversation. Then the detective shook his hand and Ronaldo slipped out the door.

Before I had time to think about what I'd seen, a young cop came up behind me and Amber. He asked to see our IDs and recorded the information in a notebook before moving on to the next person. They kept us like that, lined up against the wall, for almost 20 minutes. I wondered how long it would be before Amber lost it. Brad the bartender, who was standing next to us, also sensed her growing distress.

"You guys don't have anything to worry about," he reassured her. "They're not interested in the customers. This is happening because somebody didn't grease the right palms tonight, so it's payback. They're only going to keep you here long enough to break your balls and then they'll let everybody but the employees go, I guarantee it. I've been through this before."

And sure enough, just a few minutes later the cops started to release us in small groups. Edgar had managed to get off the DJ stage and blend into the crowd before the cops got to the back room, so he was able to walk out with the other customers when they were released. He and Amber had an emotional reunion on the sidewalk of 37th St. before I saw them into a cab and sent them on their way home.

It was beginning to get light out. I love the city at this time of day, when the streets are quiet and everything's just waking up. I decided to walk home and headed east toward 6th Avenue. All the way home I replayed the events of the night in my head, thinking about everything I'd seen and heard and trying to make sense of it all.

CHAPTER FOURTEEN

I stopped at a pay phone on the way home and called Samantha. She answered on the first ring. I don't think she ever sleeps. I picture her spending her nights hanging upside down from the rafters wrapped in her cape like some bloodsucking bat.

She did go absolutely batshit crazy when I related the events of my evening to her, She peppered me with questions and was throwing out theories faster than I could respond to them. She came at if from every angle you could think of. It was fascinating to see how her mind works, and I was beginning to understand why she'd once been such a great investigative reporter.

Who's behind the club? Is it organized crime? Who owns the building? Who has to be paid off to operate something like this and how high up does that corruption go? Who's making the payoffs? How do these pop-up operations happen, who puts them together, and how do people find out about them? And most curious of all to both of us was, What's a seemingly straight-shooting City Hall employee attached to the Mayor's office doing in an illegal after-hours club, and why did he seem to receive special treatment from the people executing the raid?

I agreed with Samantha that a lot of things didn't make sense. At one point she started to theorize that perhaps Ronaldo was there as some kind of coordinator between the mayor's office and the raid, and I interrupted her. "But if that's the case, what was he doing partying inside the club before the raid went down?" I asked her. "Besides, the mayor's office has been working exclusively with the DEA, not the local police departments." This was a deliberate choice, I knew, made to prevent the inevitable leaks that tainted locally run operations. And this raid was most definitely a local operation.

"There were no feds or DEA agents there," I told her. "Only NYPD. The bartender I talked to said the raid was payback for unmade payoffs to the local precinct." "Do you believe that?" Samantha asked. I thought about it. "He could be right. The fact that only local police were there, and the absence of any feds would support that."

"So if this Ronaldo person wasn't there in an official capacity, then what was the conversation he had with the detective all about? And why was he allowed to slip out?" Samantha shot back. I had no answer to that.

Samantha was initially upset that today's edition of the West Side News had already gone to press and she wouldn't be able to run this for another twenty-four hours. But after thinking about it, she said the extra time was actually a good thing. It would give her a chance to dig a little deeper and see what more she could find out.

"What are you looking for?" I asked her. "For starters, I want to know exactly what it is Ronaldo does at City Hall. I'm also curious about what his connection to the mayor is," she answered. "Do you think you'll find something?" "If it's the last thing I do," she said.

CHAPTER FIFTEEN

That night at work, Miguel arrived a little after ten and walked to the end of the bar. I made my way down to where he stood and said, "Hey, Mick, what's up?" He held up a copy of the West Side News. "Have you ever seen this?" he asked me Uh-oh. "What is it?' I asked.

"It's a paper called the West Side News. I found it in the waiting room at the doctor's office today. It's from a couple of weeks ago." He put it on the bar so I could see the date: October 4. The day after the OJ verdict and the day after I met Samantha and told her about Tabitha. The day my first item ran. I frantically tried to remember the wording in it, and to remember if there was anything that tied it to me..

"What were you doing at the doctor's office?" I asked, stalling for time. "Are you okay?"

Miguel scoffed, "Of course I'm okay. I took my mother there for a checkup. While I was sitting in the waiting room I picked this up to read." He opened the paper. "There's a column in here and guess what?"

"What?" I asked. I was mentally scrambling, trying to figure out where this was heading. Miguel snapped me back from my thoughts when he said, "I know this woman." I looked down. Miguel had the paper open to page 6. His finger was planted firmly on the picture of Samantha's face featured prominently at the top of her column. I tried to hide my surprise. "You know her?" I repeated. "You know Samantha Bigelow?"

"Yeah," he said. He lowered his voice. "I sell to her." Now I was really shocked. "How do you know her" I managed to ask. Miguel kept his voice low and looked around, making sure no one was near us. "Diane introduced us. She said she's a good friend of Paula's, and would I do her a favor and meet her. I'm glad I did. She's a good customer." "I've never seen her in here. Where does she buy from you?"

"I bring it to her house. She lives right down the street, on 10th, right off 6th Avenue." I knew where Samantha lived, I'd been there once myself. "Wait a minute, back up. Did you say you deliver to her?" I asked, incredulously. Miguel was notorious for keeping his life away from the bar sacrosanct. If you couldn't make it to the bar to do business with Miguel, then you didn't do business.

"I told you," he said. "She's a good customer." I took that to mean that she bought in such quantity it makes it worthwhile for Miguel to accommodate her with in-home visits. I wonder what other surprises Samantha holds? "Well, that's cool," I said, indicating the paper. I decided to rip off the band-aid. "Did you read the column?" I asked.

"No," he said, shrugging. "I looked at it but didn't really understand it, the way she writes…I thought it was stupid." He let out a hearty belly laugh. "But I found out my mother likes it. So I took this for the picture," he said folding the paper and putting it in his jacket. "I'm going to have Samantha sign it the next time I see her and give it to my mother."

I gave him a beer, and as he walked away to greet someone. I stood there with my mind spinning. What the hell was happening? I tried to sort it out. The Samantha cat was out of the bag now. Well, maybe not completely out, because Miguel hasn't connected the dots yet. Maybe I could still end all this before he ever does.

If I stop feeding Samantha items about the bar completely, that will stop any chance of a problem with Miguel ever developing. I was also thinking that with Samantha now so consumed with the ongoing Daniel Baldwin story and the breaking Ronaldo story, she'd lose interest in the penny-ante Characters stuff. Miguel would never have to be the wiser. An hour later, unfortunately, Miguel got to be the wiser.

He showed the column to somebody else in the bar, and that person actually read it. Worse, they took it upon themselves to explain the item about Tabitha to Miguel. And worse still, he told him he'd seen similar items in the same column in the past few weeks.

My first inkling that something was wrong came when I looked up to see Miguel making a beeline for the bar. I thought he looked rattled, and this piqued my curiosity, because Miguel never gets rattled. I raised my eyebrows and asked, "Hey, what's up? Is everything okay?"

"No, it's not okay at all. I'm fucking angry! Read this!" He thrust the paper at me, pointing to Samantha's column. "What?" I said, taking the paper. "You already showed me this." "Yeah but read it. Read what she wrote!" I made a show of reading the column then gave a shrug. "Yeah, you're right," I told him. "It's kinda stupid."

"Don't you see it?" he almost shouted. Realizing he was drawing attention to us, he lowered his voice and leaned into me. "She's writing about Characters! Look, right here—" He snatched the paper from my hands and read, ..."my sources tell me that she still had the magic to make it snow in October here in the West Village! What a Character!!"

"Yeah, and... What? I don't get it. She could be talking about anything; I don't see what has you so worked up." "Lookit!" he said. "Right there, 'Character" with a capital 'C', this shit about 'snow'. "And I still think they could be talking about anything," I argued. "Why do you think it's about here?"

"Because I showed it to my friend, and he told me she's been writing stuff like this in her column for weeks! He said she's always using that "What a Character" line, too! He thought I knew about it." Great, I thought! Miguel manages to talk to the one person in the city who reads this rag!

"That fucking bitch!" Miguel railed. "I'm going to kill her...And who the fuck are these 'sources' she's talking about?" Oh, shit, I thought, this is not good. I need to defuse this. "I don't know, Mick. I think your friend's got you all worked up over nothing. I mean, look at me — I just read this thing twice and still didn't get it until you pointed it out to me. And I work here! I think you're worrying over nothing, dude, I really do."

He looked at me for a long time while he processed what I'd said. Finally he said gruffly, "She still shouldn't have written this shit." "Well, I'm not going to argue with you about that," I said.

"You're right, it's fucked up. The whole thing's fucked up. Maybe you should just have a calm conversation with her about it. She obviously hasn't thought through the possible consequences for you. Explain it to her and tell her to stop." Not to mention the consequences for me if Miguel discovers my connection to it, especially after the performance I just gave. If Samantha doesn't have enough journalistic integrity to protect her source, I'm gonna have some serious 'splainin' to do.

CHAPTER SIXTEEN

As the night went on, I kept replaying over in my head the conversation I'd had with Miguel. How could I have not foreseen how this could all go so wrong? Or thought about what could happen to him? And what about Ronaldo? Is his life about to go up in flames because of what Samantha's going to write about last night?

I was in the middle of ringing up a drink when a sudden flash of clarity hit me like a thunderbolt. My actions are going to be responsible for real consequences happening to real people! This wasn't just trading salacious gossip with friends and co-workers about anonymous celebrity/strangers, these were people I knew. My hand hung suspended over the register keys as my mind raced. I'd been fucking with real lives. I felt the first unfamiliar pricks of shame, remorse, and guilt about what I was doing.

Samantha's story about Ronaldo and the after-hours club ran the next morning. If I thought that the Daniel Baldwin fallout was bad, it was nothing compared to the shitstorm unleashed by this story. Though heavy with innuendo and short on verifiable facts, she had nevertheless outdone herself, raising questions and demanding answers in a sensational column that I was sure would rock City Hall.

The reaction was immediate and explosive, and the story got picked up by various news services throughout the day. On Friday morning it landed on the front page of the Post. In the scramble to do damage control and contain the fallout, the mayor's office announced that Ronaldo Sagarro had been placed on administrative leave pending an investigation into the situation. I wondered how he was holding up under all this. Reporters descended on the apartment building down the street from me where he lives, only to find that Ronaldo was gone, and no one knows where. He seems to have gone into hiding.

I spoke to Samantha late that morning, but she cut the conversation short, telling me she was expecting company and then had a meeting at the Village Voice to prepare for. She said she'd call me later, and then hung up on me! I was pissed! I wanted to talk to her about Ronaldo, and about the Miguel situation. I thought it might be better to have that conversation in person.

CHAPTER SEVENTEEN

Samantha never called me later, but that was no surprise. I knew she wouldn't. Miguel didn't show up for work that night. This was unusual for him, but it wasn't unheard of. In his place he sent his 'cousin' who everybody called Miguelito, or 'little Miguel,' though I doubt that's his name. Little Miguel showed up about ten and told me that Miguel was sick with the bug that had been going around. He said Miguel decided to stay home and go to bed, and Miguelito would mind the business. This was no problem, as most of Miguel's customers already knew Miguelito.

On Saturday, Miguel was still sick, so Miguelito filled in for him again. That night I received back to back phone calls as soon as I started to work behind the bar. The first one came in right at eight. When I answered, a voice informed me I had a collect phone call from a state correctional facility, and would I accept the charges? I knew it was Teddy Pope, Danny's younger brother, calling me from Riker's Island,

Rikers Island is New York City's largest jail and sits in the middle of the East River between Queens and the Bronx. Technically it's not a prison, because it only holds local offenders who are either awaiting trial, serving sentences of one year or less, or are temporarily placed there pending transfer to another facility. Teddy falls into the second category. I accepted the charges and a minute later Teddy's voice came on the line.

"Yo, Billy," he said. "What's up? Is the bar busy?" "Hey, Teddy," I greeted him. "No, not really, not yet. It's still early," I said. "Is everything okay?" he asked. "None of those assholes are giving you problems, are they?"

I knew he was talking about the 'Bowery Boys' and laughed. "No, Teddy, everybody's been good, they're all on their best behavior…It's good to hear from you, dude. How's everything going for you there?" "You know, it is what it is. Are you still coming to see me next weekend?"

I'd been promising Teddy for a while that I would take the visitor's bus out to Riker's one weekend and visit him. It was the last thing on earth I wanted to do. I have an overwhelming fear of prison and being locked up, borne of an incident when I was a teenager. I'd decided after that incident that if I was ever again in the position of facing prison time, I would rather die than go to jail. But, I felt for Teddy. Plus, I owed him.

We first met about a year ago, just a few months after I'd started working at the bar. I'd heard that Danny Pope's notorious younger brother Teddy was being released on parole and I'd finally get to meet this neighborhood "legend." Four years younger than Danny, Teddy had spent 12 of his 28 years locked up. The first time I laid eyes on him, I knew immediately who he was.

I'd arrived at work and spotted him as soon as I walked in the door. He was leaning against the wall by the pool table with his feet crossed at the ankles and his hands in the pockets of his jeans. Roughly six feet tall with blonde hair and pale blue eyes, he stood stock still, but it was the stillness of a coiled snake. I watched him unobserved, with his back to the wall, not moving a muscle but completely alert.

His face was a frozen, unreadable blank mask. The only thing moving were his eyes, which never stopped darting around the room, looking everywhere at once, and taking everything in. He might as well have been wearing a sign around his neck saying, "Ex-Con, Fresh Out of the Joint." I knew that if you put a plate of food in front of this guy, he'd pick up a fork with one hand and instinctively curve his other arm protectively around the plate. This had to be Teddy Pope.

Teddy was looked up to and feared by the younger neighborhood guys. A loose knit group of second and third generation aspiring thugs, Sal referred to them affectionately as the Bowery Boys. Some of them, like Matty Payne and Jackie Maddox, I would have characterized as wannabe Westies, except the Westies no longer exist. Most of them still live at home and have a hard time finding or keeping a job.

Because some of them have felony convictions on their record, they can't apply for anything that requires a background check. Danny and Teddy Pope's Uncle Frank owns a moving company, and he throws them work when he can, but for the most part they're unemployed. Consequently, they're always scheming and planning something to make a quick buck or looking for a hustle.

I watched them huddle in a booth every night for three months, planning the robbery of a local Photomat. When they finally pulled it off, they netted thirty-six dollars to split four ways. For three months' work. And because the idiots had chosen to rob the Photomat right around the corner from where they all lived, they had to take circuitous routes home for months afterward to avoid being seen and recognized by the people they'd robbed. Not exactly master criminals.

The first few months I worked at Characters these guys were trouble. They'd come in when Sal wasn't around and try to intimidate me into giving them free drinks. They'd also try to shake down other customers for their blow, cornering them in the bathroom and basically just being all-around pains in the ass. When they heard Teddy was to be released, they were ecstatic, assuming he would fall in with them and they'd get away with anything they wanted.

So when I walked into the bar that night and saw Teddy, I knew what I had to do. I'd have no chance going up against him. My only hope of coming out on top in this was to make an ally of him. I walked behind the bar and switched out the register drawers with Diane. Then, when she headed downstairs to count her bank, I approached Teddy.

"Hey," I said. "You're Teddy, right?" I saw his eyes narrow slightly and he nodded almost imperceptibly. "I'm Billy," I continued. "Nice to meet ya. Let me buy you a drink. What are you having?" I could tell I'd thrown him off balance and could see the wheels turning in his head. "Yeah, okay," he said. "I'll have a White Russian."

A White Russian! I choked back a laugh, recognizing that that would be a big mistake. At least he didn't ask for a Grasshopper or a Pink Squirrel, but still... Hiding my surprise and amusement, I went behind the bar to make his drink. He followed me over a minute later and stood watching me. I finished shaking the drink and poured it from the cocktail shaker into the glass, stuck a straw in it and slid it across the bar to him.

"Thanks," he said, putting the straw in his mouth and drinking. "You're welcome," I said. "Welcome back. Listen, dude, whatever you want tonight is on me, to celebrate. I'll take care of you, just let me know when you're ready for another." And just like that, we were off to a great start.

As the night progressed, though, the shift turned out to be pretty stressful. I felt like I was defusing and de-escalating troublesome situations all night long, and by closing time, I had had it. I gave and served last call and was just waiting to get everybody out so I could go home and smoke a joint. The usual parade of clowns approached me after last call trying to get one more drink, but tonight I wasn't having it, and told them we were closed.

Teddy had been sitting at the bar for the last hour or so with Danny's sister-in-law Cathy O'Malley and her boyfriend Frankie One-Ball. After imbibing a steady stream of White Russians all night, he seemed to be feeling no pain. After I'd refused the fifth or sixth person trying to get "one more drink" I turned all the lights up, attempting to clear the room. All of sudden, Teddy yelled, "Billy, give me another."

I walked over to him and said quietly, "Teddy, let me get everybody out of here and I'll make you guys drinks as soon as they all leave. I've just turned down at least five people," I explained. "If they see me make you a drink, then they're all gonna want one too. Give me five minutes, okay?"

It wasn't okay. Suddenly Teddy was on his feet, his arm extended across the bar, and the barrel of a huge gun was pressing against my forehead. I don't know where he'd been carrying it, but it was out and in his hand before I knew what was happening.

"Are you disrespecting me?" he growled. "Are you fucking kidding me?" Cathy, sitting next to him, freaked out. She scooted her barstool back and screeched, "Teddy, what the fuck are you doing? He didn't do anything!" Without taking his eyes off my face, Teddy repeated, "He disrespected me."

I looked across the bar at him and finally saw the face of the person I'd heard about all these years. He had the flat cold stare of a killer. But I'd had a rough shift, I was fed up, and I'd put up with enough shit for one night. "Listen," I said to him softly, trying to keep the anger I felt out of my voice. "I've done nothing but treat you with respect and take care of you all night. You know that. I told you I'll give you another drink as soon as I get everybody out of here, but I explained that I can't make one for you when I just turned everybody else down. If you think that's disrespecting you, then you know what? Go ahead and fucking shoot me, I don't give a fuck! I am *so* over this bullshit!" And I turned my back on him and walked away.

If I'm going to be honest, as I turned my back I expected to hear the ratcheting sound of a bullet being loaded into the chamber of the gun. When I realized that wasn't going to happen, a rush of adrenaline coursed through me. I cut the jukebox and yelled to the stragglers at the tables, "We are fucking CLOSED! Everybody get the fuck out NOW! The night is over! Out! NOW! Come back tomorrow!"

The remaining customers finally took the hint and headed out the door. As the last ones left, I locked the door behind them and went back behind the bar where Teddy, Cathy and Frankie still sat. I turned the lights back down, walked up to them and said, "Now. Who wants a drink?"

After that night, Teddy became my self-appointed personal protector. He told Cathy he was completely flipped out that a little gay guy (I'm pretty sure he used a different term) stood up to him like that. I had unwittingly managed to win his respect and he became both my ally and my advocate. One night he heard the Bowery Boys hatching a plan to get drinks from me without paying and he shut them down. Miguel told me he overheard Teddy say to them, "Listen, you assholes don't fuck with Billy anymore! He's a standup guy. From now on, if you fuck with him, you're fucking with me! You got that?"

And that's all it took. My life at the bar changed overnight. Nobody fucked with me anymore and, in fact, everybody started watching my back. Even when Teddy got violated for a bar fight on 14th St. and sent back to finish his sentence, his influence remained.

I was "Teddy's Boy." Everyone knew he called me regularly from Riker's and was being kept in the loop. They also knew he'd be out again one day, and nobody wanted to be looking over their shoulder when that happened.

So, like I said, I owed him. "Yeah," I said, "I'll be there on Saturday." "Oh, that's great!" he said. "Hey, did you ask Irene about that other thing?" We knew his phone calls were recorded. He had to be careful with what he said, and it took me a minute to figure out what he was talking about.

He had told me that when his brother Danny was in Riker's, Danny's wife Irene had successfully passed him a small glassine envelope of cocaine on visiting day. Teddy had asked me to find out from Irene how she'd done it, so I could get something to him.

"Yeah," I told him, "I asked her." "Yeah? And...?" "She had it in her mouth." I told him. "When she greeted him, she gave him a big, wet, sloppy kiss, and slipped it to him with her tongue." I paused, waiting to see what he'd say. "Waddya think?" I asked, trying not to laugh.

There was dead silence on the other end of the line. "Yeah, no, that's not gonna work...yeah, no, never mind, dude, let's just forget about it I guess..." "Yeah, that's probably best," I said. "I'll bring some money to put in your commissary account, though, and if you think of anything else you want or need that they'll let me bring in, let me know by Friday."

"Okay, that sounds good. Thanks, Billy..." We talked for a few more minutes, but the bar was starting to get busy, so I told him I had to go and I'd see him next Saturday. I no sooner hung up the phone when it rang again. I picked it up. "Hello, Characters!' I answered. "Hey, Billy, it's me," said Jeremy. I was struck briefly by how surreal my life had become. Who gets phone calls at work from convicts and pop stars? One calls from a prison, the other from a movie set.

With everything that had been going on, I'd completely forgotten that Jeremy was coming back this week. "Jeremy! What's up?" I said. "Oh, man, I'm glad you called. What day are you getting back?" "Well, yeah, that's what I'm calling to tell you," he answered. "I won't be back this week after all. I just got cast in a movie with Christian Slater and have to fly right to that location from here."

"Oh, that sucks!" I moaned. "Not that you got the movie, that's great! Congratulations! I'm just bummed that you won't be back." Down the bar, someone was trying to catch my eye, waving an empty glass in the air and pointing at it. "Look, J.," I said, "I can't talk right now, people are getting pissed. Give me a number that I can reach you at tomorrow." He rattled off a number that I wrote on an envelope beside the register. After telling him I'd call him in the morning, I hung up.

The bar had filled while I was on the phone, and I had to kick it into gear to get caught up. Speaking of the Devil, the Bowery Boys put in an appearance but didn't stay long. The usual crowd was out in force, including Buzzy, Brania, Black Lil and Fat Sara. Around three A.M. my friend Erik Engstrom showed up with someone I didn't recognize.

In addition to being one of the nicest people I know, Erik is hot: he's tall and well built, with a head of curly blond hair and an open boyish face. His father is the Swedish ambassador to Kenya. I've been friends with Erik for four or five months, since he first arrived in New York from Sweden to study photography and graphic design. He's another one of those people who just happened into the bar one night by chance and became an instant regular. He's funny, completely crazy, and I always end up laughing my ass off when I'm with him. He's become a good friend; one I hang out with outside the bar.

On this night, he came in the door, lifted me off my feet in a bear hug and spun me around. Putting me down, he asked for two Heinekens and turned to the guy he came in with. "Billy, I want you to meet my friend, Alexander Tolstoy. Call him Alex." I put a Heineken down in front of him and said, "Nice to meet you, Alex. Any relation to Leo?" I laughed.

"He was my great-grandfather," Alex replied. What? "Really?" Erik answered for him, "Yes, really." I looked at Alex. "Leo Tolstoy, the author of 'War and Peace,' is your great-grandfather." Alex just shrugged and nodded. No big deal.

"Well, nice to meet you," I said. Movie stars, convicts, pop stars, strippers, and now Leo Tolstoy's great-grandson. I wondered, who else is going to walk into this place? I wiped the bar down in front of them, where they took two stools. "Where are you guys coming from tonight?" I asked them. "Alex's father's house," Erik answered. "He's a lawyer."

"Here in New York?" I asked. "Everywhere," answered Alex. My confusion must have shown on my face because Erik chimed in. "He's a big international lawyer. He defended Noriega." I looked at Alex with raised eyebrows, and he confirmed Erik's statement with another shrug and a nod. Alex seemed to be big on the 'shrug and nod' method of communication.

"So," Erik continued, "we were hanging out in his father's library tonight and I saw this sitting on his desk." He opened his wallet and pulled out a laminated card, a little smaller than an index card. Handing it to me, he said, "I asked Alex if we could bring it here so I could show it to you. I knew you'd get a kick out of it."

I took the card and looked at it. Printed across the top it read "Personal Numbers I Need to Know." I looked down and saw a list of five people, each name followed by a phone number prefaced by its international calling code. I read the names and my eyes widened in surprise. Printed on the card were the names and numbers of Manuel Noriega, President Bill Clinton, Soviet Premier Boris Yeltsin, Queen Elizabeth, and Pope John Paul II! I looked at them.

"Is this for real?" I asked. Erik nodded yes, smiling. Alex said, "Those are their personal numbers. Direct lines, I believe." "Holy crap." I said, "this is awesome!" I looked at Alex. "Can I copy these numbers? Please, this would be so cool to have."

Alex smiled and said, "Sure, I just need to bring back the original card. Go ahead and copy the numbers if you want, I don't mind." I'm not sure his father would have felt the same way, but I didn't care.

I copied the numbers and gave him back the card. Taking the time difference into consideration, I did some quick math and figured it would just be coming up on lunchtime in England when I finished work. I decided I'd "ring up" Buckingham Palace and see what happens.

CHAPTER EIGHTEEN

The line was busy. I'd started calling Queen Elizabeth's direct line in Buckingham Palace as soon as I'd gotten home from work, and for almost two hours had gotten nothing but a busy signal. Who the hell is Queenie talking to, I wondered?

I hung up from my latest attempt. My hand was still resting on the receiver when the phone rang beneath it, startling me. I looked at the clock, wondering who the hell was calling me this early in the morning. "Hello?" I answered.

"Billy, it's me," I heard Miguel say. "Miguel?" What the fuck? "How are you feeling, are you still sick?" Ignoring my question, he asked, "Have you seen the Post today?" "The Post?" I said. "No, it wasn't out yet when I came home. Why, what's in the Post?" I asked him. This can't be good if Miguel is calling me at 7 o'clock in the morning I thought.

"It's Samantha," he said. My stomach sank. "Oh, no," I said to him. "What'd she do now?" "She's dead." he said. "She was murdered!" "What?!? Murdered! How? What happened?" "Her landlady found her in her apartment last night. It says it looks like

Samantha might have interrupted a robbery." "Oh my god," I said. "That's horrible! Does it say how she was killed?"

"No, it doesn't go into a lot of detail. It just says that the landlady had noticed Samantha's door had been ajar most of the day, and when she finally decided to check it out, she found Samantha's body. They think she was probably killed sometime Friday." "Do they have any leads, any idea who did it?" "No, or if they do, they're not saying anything yet. When was the last time you talked to her?"

I thought back to my last phone conversation with Samantha when she'd hung up on me. But wait a minute! Why was Miguel asking me when I'd last spoken to her? Miguel wasn't supposed to know anything about my connection to her. "What are you talking about?" I asked. "Why would I have talked to her? I didn't even know her."

"Oh, of course," he said. "I forgot." He paused, then said, "I wonder if it wasn't a robbery." "What do you mean?" I asked cautiously. "What if Samantha wasn't the accidental victim of a robbery? What if she was targeted?" "Targeted!" I said. "You mean because of something she wrote about?" "I bet that story she broke about the guy from City Hall and the after-hours club pissed off a lot of people. The kind of people you don't want to piss off." "So you're saying you think one of her stories might have had something to do with what happened to her?" The phone was silent as Miguel thought about it. "I don't know," he replied. "I just hope they find out who did it, and they find out fast."

I knew what he meant. An investigation into Samantha's life was bound to reveal things that neither Miguel nor I wanted known. My mind was spinning. Would they think that something I'd passed on to Samantha had something to do with her murder? Or would they think it was completely unrelated, just a random act of violence in a robbery gone wrong?

I tried to think of anything that might come up in an investigation that would connect me with Samantha. We spoke on the phone frequently, but I made most of my calls to her from the pay phone at the bar. She had been calling me quite a bit lately, calls I did take on the phone behind the bar. But that was the same phone line as the extension on the desk in the basement. The police would probably discover that she was friends with both Paula and Diane, and with any luck they would think it was one of them she was calling.

"Billy, are you there?" I heard Miguel asking through the receiver. "Yeah, sorry, just thinking…. What about you, did you go see her after you saw her column?" I remembered how worked up he was Wednesday night about what she'd written. I wanted to ask him if he'd followed through with his plan to confront her but couldn't figure out how to ask him that without sounding accusatory. I got my answer anyway.

"No," he said, "that was the day I woke up feeling so sick, so I never saw her." Neither one of us said anything for a minute. I knew I was missing something, but I couldn't put my finger on what it was. I needed time to think. "Listen, Mick, " I said, "I'm gonna go down and grab a paper. This shit is crazy. Are you gonna be around tonight?" "Yeah," he said, "I'm feeling all better now, I'll be in." "Okay, I'll see you then," I said, but he had already hung up.

CHAPTER NINETEEN

Miguel's phone call put all thoughts of calling the Queen out of my mind. As soon as I hung up, I grabbed my jacket and ran downstairs to buy a Post. The New York Post is the city's leading tabloid, famous for its outrageous, and often hilarious headlines. One of its most famous heralded the discovery of a decapitated corpse in a strip club. The headline trumpeted "HEADLESS BODY IN TOPLESS BAR."

My personal favorite was when the husband of Carol Channing, beloved star of "Hello Dolly!" revealed that he and his famous wife hadn't had sex in forty years! In letters six inches high that filled the entire top half of the front page, the Post headline blared "HELL NO, DOLLY!"

When I read the Post, I'm reminded of a Ron Howard-directed movie called "The Paper." In the movie, Michael Keaton's character works for the tabloid, and is offered a job with the New York Times. "Just think," says the guy trying to convince him to take the job, "you'll be reporting on the entire world!"

"I don't live in the world," Keaton shoots back. "I live in New York City!" That's the way I feel. If you live in New York City, the New York Post is the only newspaper you need to read. The Post covers *my* world. It's my Bible. Well actually, TV Guide is my Bible, but the Post runs a close second. Unfortunately, on that morning, the Post let me down. After reading their article about Samantha's murder, I didn't know any more than I had before. I did know somebody, though, who might be able to get more information.

In the early '90s I worked briefly as a private eye for Eddie Murphy. Not Eddie Murphy the movie star, but Eddie Murphy the Irish, gay, retired NYC police detective who now runs his own private investigation agency. He also worked security on Friday nights at Roebling's, the restaurant in the South Street Seaport where I worked in the eighties, and where we first met.

Eddie had approached me one day and asked if I'd be interested in helping him out with a case he was working on. As a kid I was obsessed with Dick Tracy and the Hardy Boys, even buying The Hardy Boys' Detective Handbook and studying it like the Bible (or the TV Guide). Eddie told me that if I liked the job, I could work for him for two years and then apply for my own private investigator's license. Since the acting career I'd moved to New York to pursue was stalled (alright, non-existent), I said I'd love to try it and see what happens.

Unfortunately, the job didn't work out and I abandoned my dream of becoming the third Hardy Boy. But Eddie and I remained good friends and occasionally would meet up for a drink.

When Eddie worked for the NYPD, it was out of the 6th precinct, the precinct I knew was handling Samantha's case. Being pretty sure he still has contacts there who could tell him more about the investigation than I was reading in the paper, I called and asked him if he could meet me for a drink that afternoon.

I told him I had something I wanted to talk to him about and suggested we meet at Hogs and Heifers, a dive bar located in the old meatpacking district on 13th and Washington St., near the Hudson river. Hogs and Heifers caters to bikers and is known for its display of the hundreds of bras that hang behind the bar, all donated by inebriated patrons. I was friendly with Chrissy, one of the bartenders there. Chrissy is tiny and very pretty, with a wild mass of curly black hair that contrasts dramatically with her alabaster skin. She has the sweet innocent face and manner of a young girl, but I happen to know that that belies the tough woman she is underneath.

I got to Hogs and Heifers for my meeting with Eddie and found the place closed to the public for the afternoon. As the security guy stood in the doorway explaining this to me, I heard Chrissy's voice from inside the bar yell, "Billy, is that you?" I saw her come from behind the bar and approach the door.

"He's okay," she told the bouncer. "That's Billy, from Characters. Let him in." "What's going on?" I asked Chrissy, returning the hug she gave me. "Playboy magazine is doing a photo shoot here until 5. Come on in and check it out. Let me get you a drink-" I looked around and noticed for the first time the lights and various pieces of equipment set up around the pool table and other parts of the bar. Someone with a light meter was checking settings while I saw another guy fussing with cameras. Numerous well-endowed models in varying stages of undress lounged around, waiting to resume the shoot.

"I was supposed to meet somebody here," I told Chrissy. I turned from her in time to observe Eddie through the window, approaching the door. "That's him at the door now," I said.

Chrissy turned and yelled, "Yo, Joey, let that guy in!" Eddie entered and crossed the room to where I was standing at the bar. I introduced him to Chrissy, who asked him what he was drinking. He told her a Budweiser. She got my Jack on the rocks and Eddie's beer, putting them on the bar in front of us. When I went to pull out my wallet, she said, "Oh, no, sweetie, there's no charge today. Technically, we're closed, and this is a private function. Playboy's paying for everything, so drink up."

We picked up our drinks, thanked her, and drifted over toward the pool table. I put my glass on a wooden ledge on the wall and leaned back to watch the photographer composing his shot. He was draping the now topless models across the pool table while others posed behind them holding pool cues. "Well, this is different," Eddie said, taking in the scene.

"I know, huh? Thanks for coming, man, I'm glad you were free." "No problem. What did you want to talk to me about?" I took a fortifying gulp of my drink. "I was thinking about hiring you." Eddie looked at me askance. "Hiring me? What do you want to hire me to do?"

I looked around to make sure no one could overhear us. Nobody was paying any attention to us anyway. Why would they, with all the other stuff that was going on? "Did you read the Post today?" I asked him. He was raising his beer to his mouth. He paused and looked at me, nodding. "Did you happen to read the story about the writer Samantha Bigelow who got murdered?"

He finished bringing the beer to his mouth and drank before answering. "Yeah," he said, staring at the girls around the pool table. "Somewhere here in the West Village, wasn't it? Tenth St., I think." He turned and looked at me. "What about it?" I pondered how much to tell him. I finally figured I should just be honest with him and lay out the whole situation. I told him how Samantha had recruited me and my participation in the items in her column, culminating with my involvement in the latest Ronaldo Sagarro fiasco.

"Wow, that was you?" he said when I finished. "Yeah, and now she's dead, and I don't have any idea why. Was it a robbery gone bad, or is it something else? I'm scared shitless that one of these things she printed pissed off the wrong person and that's what got her killed. I need you to find out what happened." "Billy, you know I can't get involved in a case that has an active police investigation going on."

"Well, if you can't work the case, can you at least find out what the police are maybe thinking and doing? I'm not even sure how she was killed. You must know somebody who can tell you something...." He looked at me pensively for a minute, then handed me his empty bottle. "Here," he said. "Go get another one of these free beers for me and let me make a phone call." He headed toward the bathrooms where the pay phone was, and I made my way back to the bar. Almost ten minutes passed before he joined me, taking the stool next to mine. Reaching for his new beer, he brought it to his mouth and took a long pull on it.

"Well, you lucked out," he told me. "Turns out my old partner, Gene Rame, is the one who caught the case." "Did you talk to him?' I asked. "Yeah. He couldn't say much, but I found out a few things." He took another drink and swiveled his stool to face me. "He did tell me the cause of death was strangulation." "Strangulation?" I said. "I thought one of the papers said she was killed by a blow to the head."

"That's what they thought at first, and it was more like multiple blows. But the autopsy showed she'd been strangled to death before her head was bashed in. They haven't released that information. They also haven't found the weapon used to beat her head in. The ME said there were tiny glass fragments in the wounds, making them think a heavy glass object was used."

"What else did he tell you?" Eddie looked around again to make sure no one was within earshot. "The whole robbery thing is just something they floated to the press. Gene says they're pretty sure she knew her killer." "Why do they think that?"

"Well, for one thing, there was no sign of forced entry. They think Samantha must have let in whoever killed her. Also, she had a safe that was wide open when she was found. It doesn't make sense that she would have had the safe open with someone she didn't know in the apartment." "But was she robbed?" I asked.

"Well, here's the thing. There were things missing – the police didn't find any files, notebooks, or papers anywhere, which is strange, considering she's a writer. Her purse was there, but no wallet or any kind of identification, and jewelry and silver, you know, stuff you can pawn, was all left behind." He took another drink. "Gene said it felt personal to him. Whoever did this bashed her head to a bloody pulp after they strangled her. It was overkill. That kind of viciousness usually indicates the victim knew their killer." I mulled all this over and finally looked up at Eddie. "What do you think I should do here?"

"Nothing," he answered. "Wait and see how it plays out. I have no doubt that once they get her phone records someone will be coming around to check you out. But right now, I don't think you really have anything that would contribute to the investigation. Anyone you might have tipped her off about has already been written about and 'exposed,' so you don't know anything that they're not already privy to, right?'"

I tried to think of anything I could tell him and came up blank. "I am right, aren't I?" Eddie persisted. "You don't know anything that you haven't told me, do you? If you do, tell me now…" "No," I assured him, "I've told you everything I can about all of this." Well, almost everything. I hadn't mentioned Miguel. "I wonder, though, if this might be connected to whatever it was that Samantha was so jacked about recently. She kept bringing up something she was working on that could lead to big things for her. It was connected to some old co-worker of hers from the Village Voice, I think. In fact, the last time I talked to her on the phone she rushed me off because she had an appointment with somebody from the Voice that she had to get ready for."

"Mmm," said Eddie, "did she tell you who she was meeting with?" "No," I said, "and I have no way to find something like that out." I looked at him. "Maybe you could find out who she was talking to at the Voice from your friend. It would probably show in her phone records when they get them, don't you think?"

"Yeah, most likely, something would be there, but I've got no basis for getting that information from Gene." "C'mon, Eddie, I know you can think of a way to find out. Do me a favor, just think about it, okay? If you could find out what she was working on for them, it might just point in the direction of the killer." And point away from me. "Hell, tell your buddy Gene the truth about why you want to know, they should be investigating that anyway. But please, you have to keep me out of it. A lot of people are going to be really angry if it comes out that I was the one giving Samantha that stuff. I don't want to end up like she did, with my head bashed in." Eddie shook his head and looked at the floor. "Let me see what I can do," he said, and then we went back to watching naked women shoot pool for the rest of the afternoon.

CHAPTER TWENTY

The next morning, I had to go to the Jefferson Market Library to return some books. The library, which sits on 10th Street between Greenwich Avenue and 6th Avenue, is one of my favorite buildings in the city. Built in the late 1800s, the Victorian Gothic structure was originally a courthouse and was erected with an adjacent prison and market. Sometime in the 1920's the prison and market were torn down and replaced with the Women's House of Detention. The original building was empty and abandoned by 1958, and in 1967 was converted into a library. In 1973 the prison addition was torn down and replaced by a beautiful community garden.

Ordinarily I would spend some time in the library when I went there. It had an interior that reminded me of a castle, complete with a winding stone staircase leading up to a circular tower at the top. I loved wandering through its various rooms with their unexpected nooks and crannies, lit through stained glass windows and covered in warm wood paneling. But today I was on a mission. After I dropped the books off I was going to detour down 10th Street and check out the building where Samantha was killed.

I had a semblance of a plan, but first I had to pick up a Village Voice. I crossed 6th Avenue and went up to the news store on the corner of 11th St. to buy a paper and a red marker. I folded the paper open to the real estate section and circled some random ads in the rental listings. I walked down a block to 10th St and turned left, heading toward 5th Avenue.

I spotted Samantha's building halfway down the block on the north side of the street. As I drew near, an elderly man emerged from the alley next to the building. He was pushing a hand dolly on which a trash can balanced precariously. The poor guy looked to be about eighty years old. He was trying to navigate the dolly to the curb but seemed to be struggling. Could this be the building super? I'd been hoping to find someone to talk to in the building, and the super was as good as anybody.

"Excuse me," I called to him, "Do you need a hand?" He stopped and turned. "No, I've got it. I just need to get it over this little hump." I crossed over to him and grabbed the top of the trash can, steadying it for him as he deposited it into place. After extracting the dolly from underneath, he straightened up to look at me. "Thanks," he said, dusting off his hands. "That curb seems to get farther away every week."

I laughed, and said, "Can I ask you something?" I held up the paper I was holding and pretended to look at one of my circled ads. "Do you know where Patchin Place is?" I asked. He turned around and pointed back in the direction I'd come from. "Yeah", he said, "it's right up the street. You're on the wrong side of 6th Avenue." He pointed west up 10th St. "It's right on the other side of 6th. There's a gate on the right-hand side of the sidewalk, and it's the cul-de-sac behind the gate. If you hit Homer's Diner you've passed it."

"Oh," I said, "I know exactly where you mean. I walked right by it." I looked past him to the building we stood in front of. "Are you the super here?" I asked. "I'm the landlord," he replied. Oh, even better, I thought. "My name is Billy. I'm on an apartment hunt," I said, offering my hand. "I'm Fred," he said, taking my hand and shaking it. "My wife and I bought this building back in 1943." "1943? Wow! You guys are like neighborhood fixtures, huh?"

He chuckled and said, "Yeah, you could say that I guess." "I would love to live in this neighborhood." I told him. "Do you happen to know of any apartments for rent? Is there anything available in this building?" "Funny you should ask," he said. He took a handkerchief out of his pocket and wiped the back of his neck. He turned from me and looked up at his building. "We only have twelve units in the building, and all our tenants have been here for years. Some for decades." He turned his head to look at me. "Just so happens, one of the apartments is opening up."

"Really?" I said. "You mean, you actually have something available? Right now?" "Well, not exactly," he said, "but soon." He looked around and stepped in close to me. "We've had a tragedy recently. The tenant in 2C died, but I'm not sure when the apartment's going to be available to rent." "Oh, I'm so sorry," I said. "Did the tenant die in the apartment? Not that that would bother me —" Fred looked away. He hitched up his pants and cleared his throat.

"Yes," he finally said. "She died upstairs. The police are involved so we have to wait for them to release the apartment to us before we can think about renting it. We're going to have a big cleanup to do, and of course we'll have to repaint." He turned to me. "I suppose I should tell you now, since you're bound to find out anyway. The woman who lived there was murdered."

"Murdered!" I said, feigning shock. "What happened? Do they know who did it?" "Not yet." he answered. "I've gotta tell you, everybody's a little shook up. Like I said, we're a quiet building, everybody knows everybody, at least by sight and to say 'Hi' to…" "And nobody saw or heard anything?"

"Well, my wife's the one who found the body," Fred confided. "On Friday she went up to visit with her friend Minnie in 2B after lunch and noticed that Samantha's door was ajar when she left. Samantha, that's the tenant in 2C. Then on Saturday she saw the door was still ajar and decided to investigate. She walked in and found a bloody mess." He shook his head. "That poor woman," he said.

I wondered if he was talking about Samantha or his wife. "And nobody saw anything funny or heard anything? Maybe noticed somebody around who shouldn't have been here?" "As a matter of fact," Fred said, scratching his chin. "Minnie mentioned she passed someone on the stairs Friday afternoon when she was coming back from Balducci's. She was complaining to the wife about how this guy almost knocked her over coming out the front door."

Now that's interesting, I thought. "Did she tell the police about him?" "I don't know, I guess so. I know they talked to her, they talked to everyone in the building, so I imagine she told them about him. Don't know how much good that did. All she remembered was that the guy had a mustache and was carrying something. I don't see that being much help."

A mustache? My mind immediately went to Ronaldo and his new mustache, and Miguel, who also has one. But Minnie said she saw this guy on Friday afternoon, and that was the day Miguel was supposedly laid up with the bug. "Did she tell you anything else about this guy?" I asked Fred. "His hair color, height, weight?" "He had dark hair, she said, and he was tall." He laughed. "Of course, Minnie's only 4'10", so she thinks everybody's tall."

"Anybody else?" I asked. "Did any of your other tenants see anything or hear something maybe?" Fred looked at me with a frown. Was he getting suspicious of all my questions? "No, not that I heard about, anyway. Like I said, it was a complete shock to us all," he said. "It's a shame, she was a good tenant."

I thought it prudent to wrap this up. Frankly, I was kind of surprised I'd gotten as much out of him as I had. I smiled and said, "Well, it was nice talking to you, Fred. Maybe I'll see you again-" "What about the apartment?" he said. "I don't know when it's gonna be available, but are you interested?" "Uh, yeah, maybe. I want to check out this listing on Patchin Place," I said. I handed him the red marker I'd bought and the newspaper. "Why don't you write down your number and I'll give you a call in a couple of days to see where things stand."

He wrote down the phone number and handed the paper back to me. "If I'm not there my wife will be able to tell you what's going on. I'll tell her to expect a call from you so she'll know who you are. It's Billy, right?" "Yeah, that'd be great, Fred," I replied. "What's your wife's name?" "Ethel," he answered. Of course it is.

CHAPTER TWENTY-ONE

I thought it was time to talk to Diane. The fact that Miguel had asked me when I'd last talked to Samantha still weighed on me. I needed to know if Miguel knew that I was the one feeding Samantha stories.

Initially I thought Samantha was the only person who could have told him. I'd forgotten that there was someone else who knew about my connection to Samantha and that was the person who'd introduced me to her: Diane.

When I got to Characters, I found Diane reading the Post at the far end of the bar next to the ice machine. There were a couple of construction workers having a liquid lunch at the other end of the bar, closest to the door. Old Man Eddie occupied his usual seat at the banquette, on the other side of the ice machine from where Diane was standing. His pitcher of draft beer sat on the table before him.

As I approached, Diane folded the paper. "Hey Eddie," she said, "Ya want the Post?" Eddie got up and shuffled over to pick up the paper. I slid onto the end barstool and asked Diane for a

Coke. "How ya doing, Eddie?" I asked the old man as he turned and sat back down on the banquette. "Better than that Samantha Bigelow dame," he said. I looked at Diane and gave her a "what the fuck?" look. She locked eyes with me. "Eddie and I were just talking about Samantha's murder," she said carefully, holding my gaze. "He remembered seeing her in here a few weeks ago." "In here?" I said.

"Yeah," Eddie piped up. "You were here. I saw Diane introduce you to her. And she locked the key in the bathroom, dontcha remember? What's the matter, Tiddlywinks, you getting senile already?" He started to cackle at his own wit, but it caught in his throat and turned into a rattling, phlegmy cough. When it subsided, he took a swallow of his beer and lit a cigarette.

That's great, I thought. Another person who can tie me to Samantha and who talks to Miguel.... The construction workers at the end of the bar signaled to Diane and she walked down to replenish the drinks sitting in front of them. She returned and started to wipe the bar down with a bar rag. "Have you heard anything about it?" I asked her. "Anything that hasn't been in the papers?"

"No, neither Paula nor I has heard a thing," she replied. "In fact," she continued, "we hadn't talked to her or seen her in, gee, I don't know, a couple of weeks maybe? It's just so disturbing. Poor Paula's really upset. They'd known each other for so long...." She trailed off, staring into the distance at nothing. She shook off whatever it was she'd been thinking about and looked at me. "What about you?" she asked. "What have you heard?"

"Nothing. Nothing at all. Have the police contacted either you or Paula for an interview?" "No," Diane said. "Why? Do you think they will?" "Unless they find the guy who broke in there and did this and solve this thing right away then, yeah, I think they're going to want to talk to everybody. I don't know how close you guys all were, but I imagine that when they check her phone records, they'll want to talk to the people she's been in contact with."

Diane was quiet. She was slowly nodding her head as she thought about what I'd said. "Hey, Tiddlywinks," Eddie called out. "If you're done gossiping over there like an old woman, you wanna let me beat you in a game of pool?" "Sure," I said. "rack 'em up!"

We'd only started playing when Diane called to me that she was going downstairs to see Paula for a minute and asked me to keep an eye on things. "No problem," I replied as the basement door swung shut behind her. Eddie straightened up from the table where he'd just missed a shot and reached for the chalk. I leaned over to line up with the cue ball and he circled behind me, chalking his cue.

Just as I went to shoot, he said, "She's lyin', ya know." I straightened up without shooting and turned to look at him. "Who, Diane?" I asked. "Of course, Diane, who else have you been talking to? Geez, Tiddlywinks, sometimes I wonder about you." "What do you mean 'she's lying?' What's she lying about?" "Ha!" Eddie barked. "Who knows, prob'ly everything! But just now she lied to you about not seeing that Samantha Bigelow in a couple of weeks."

"What are you talking about?" I asked. Old Man Eddie was known for stirring the pot whenever he had a chance. He loved nothing more than instigating and agitating, then sitting back to enjoy the results of his efforts.

"I'm talking about that woman, that Samantha Bigelow, was in here Thursday afternoon. She was downstairs with Paula for over an hour, and when she left, she huffed right past Diane without a word." "And this was on Thursday, of last week?" I asked him. "How do you remember that it was Thursday? Hell, Old Man, you can't even remember what happened yesterday most of the time."

Eddie stepped in and got right in my face. He kept his voice low, but the anger in it spoke volumes. "Listen, you little shit, I get a lot of crap from people in this place, and I put up with most of it, too. But I don't wanna hear it from you. When you do it, it means something, because I know you know better."

I was completely taken aback. "I'm sorry, Eddie," I said. "I was just breaking your balls. I didn't mean anything by it. You know that." Eddie stepped back and gave a begrudging shrug. "Yeah, I know that. You and me, we break each other's balls, I know you don't mean it. But a lot of people here treat me like some kind of joke, or a punchline." He picked up the chalk and resumed chalking his cue. "But sometimes, the joke's on them. They act like I'm not even here, like I don't see and hear things.... But I do, and when they figure that out, then they'll see…"

"So back to my question. How do you remember it was Thursday that you saw Samantha?" "Because it was the day before all the other stuff happened, and that was Friday." Now I was completely confused. "Eddie," I said, "what the hell are you talking about? What happened Friday?"

Eddie cast a glance toward the closed basement door and lowered his voice. "I got over here early, about eleven thirty. So I went to Papa's Place to get a coffee and sit in the window until

Diane opened up." Papa's Place is the ice cream parlor style restaurant at 13th and 6th, across the street from Characters.

"And what happened?" I asked. "Right after I sat down with my coffee, I saw Diane coming out of the bar. She pulled the gate back across the door and locked it. Then she took off down 6th Avenue." "And...?" I prompted.

"And by the time she comes back and unlocks the gate and the door, it was almost an hour later! A minute after she went inside, all the neon lights and signs came on, so I paid for my coffee and went over."

"That's it? Maybe she just had to run an errand or take care of something she forgot about before work. Did you ask her?" "Yeah, I asked her. I asked her why she was late, and she said she overslept. You know, like she just got here from home." "Maybe you misunderstood what she meant. What else happened?" I asked. "Sal showed up with Sonny about an hour later," Eddie continued, his eyes now darting over to the basement door nervously. "They went right downstairs. Five minutes later he calls up Diane on the phone and tells her to come downstairs."

"Yeah, and what happened?" I pressed him. "Two minutes later, Diane comes back up. She's carrying some kind of a - it looked like a white plastic bag that had something rolled up in it and was all wrapped in duct tape. She went behind the bar and buried it in the trash can next to the ice machine, covering it over with the garbage that was in there."

I remembered Fred telling me about the man Minnie had seen coming out of Samantha's building. She said he was tall, with a mustache, and carrying "something." Sal had a mustache, but wasn't particularly tall, although Minnie was only 4'10", so who knows what "really tall" is to her. But as hard as I tried, I couldn't think of any connection Sal could have to any of this.

"And Diane did all this right in front of you?" I asked him. "No, it wasn't right in front of me. I could see her in the mirror. But like I told ya, these people don't even notice me. They act like I'm part of the furniture. That's what happens when you get old, Tiddlywinks. You get invisible." I listened to what he was saying and, sadly, recognized the truth in his words.

"Don't look so sad, Kiddo," Eddie said. "There's an upside to all that. It means they're always going to underestimate you. For instance, think how surprised Diane would be if she knew that as soon as she went to the Ladies' Room I dug out the package she'd buried in the trashcan, hid it under my coat and took it home."

At that moment, the basement door opened, and Diane came back into the room. She went back behind the bar without saying anything to us, and Eddie and I continued with our game of pool. Probably because I was so distracted by the conversation we'd just had, Eddie beat me handily, but rather than gloating and ribbing me as he usually would, he shut down. He went back to his table and sat down, opened the Post he'd gotten from Diane and buried his face in it. I took the hint. I knew he wasn't going to be telling me anything else today, so I said goodbye to both of them and headed home.

CHAPTER TWENTY-TWO

The next week was relatively uneventful. Another bar in the West Village was raided by the DEA. When I heard about it I thought of Samantha and realized how relieved I was to know she wouldn't be printing any more items about Characters. Then I felt guilty.

Paula and Diane had both been interviewed by the police once they'd gotten Samantha's phone records, but it seemed I was still flying under the radar. Just as I'd hoped, the detectives working the case assumed the calls to and from the bar were all between Samantha, Diane, and Paula. My connection to her had so far gone undetected.

Old Man Eddie continued to avoid me and deflected any attempts I made to get more information from him. I touched base with Eddie Murphy who told me the police were sifting through dozens of people Samantha had had connections to, including people at City Hall. It seems Samantha had made a lot of enemies over the years. The suspect pool was dauntingly large, and with no real leads it was going to take some time for the investigators to narrow it down.

In the meantime, things at the bar went on as usual. One night, Chris Lazar, a lawyer who spends his workdays in the courtrooms on Centre St. walked in the door. He asked for a shot of tequila before he even had his coat off. I'm not sure what kind of law Chris practices. Based on the fact he's always wearing one of two cheap suits and his personal grooming habits leave something to be desired, I've concluded that he either works for the Public Defender's Office or he's one of those struggling bottom feeders who troll the courtroom hallways trying to hustle business. I'm leaning toward the latter.

Brania came over to join him from her seat at the other end of the bar. Brania had been a 'rope dancer' at Studio 54 in the early '80's, one of those people who hung and spun on ropes suspended from the ceiling. She predictably aged out of that profession, and now works for a big travel agency, booking and coordinating international junkets for large groups and corporations. She still maintains the killer body of an athlete though. I know that she and Chris have been hooking up for a while, but they think it's a secret. I don't have the heart to tell them that everybody knows, and nobody cares.

"Rough day?" she asked Chris as I poured his tequila. "Every day!" he said before throwing down the shot. He squeezed his eyes shut and pointed to his glass, indicating I should refill it. I reached for the tequila bottle and said, "Hey Chris, remember the story you told me about that psycho judge you always appear in front of in Family Court?"

"Oh, God, which story? There are so many…" "This was about a lawyer with a ponytail," I prodded him. "Oh, the lawyer with the ponytail! I remember. I told you about that?" "Yeah, the day it happened." I turned to Brania. "Did you ever hear this story?" She shook her head 'no.' "That judge is fucking crazy!" Chris said. "You know, come to think of it, I haven't seen her around in a while."

Brania looked at him. "What happened to the lawyer with the ponytail?" He took another gulp of tequila and turned to face her. "I was appearing in front of her in Family Court and the other lawyer had this ponytail. He's talking, and all of a sudden she stops him mid-sentence and tells him to approach the bench." "The other lawyer?" Brania asked.

"Yeah. She tells him to approach her and turn around. So he does, and as soon as he turns his back to her she picks up this big pair of scissors and chops the guy's fucking ponytail right off! Right there in the courtroom in front of everybody!" "Oh my God!" Brania cried. "She didn't!"

"Oh, yes she did!" he said, starting to laugh. "And wait, it gets better! She hangs the ponytail off the back of her chair, like it's a fucking scalp, and then, she tells him to proceed. Like nothing happened! That guy was so rattled...Imagine trying to argue your case while you're looking at your scalp hanging off the judge's chair!" He laughed. "It was the easiest case I ever won, but man, I felt so sorry for that poor bastard...." He looked at me. "What the hell made you think of that?"

"Well, I think I saw her today," I told him. "Who?" Chris asked. "The judge?" I nodded. "What do you mean 'you saw her?' Where'd you see her?" "On TV," I told him. "She has her own TV show now, it just started. It's called 'Judge Judy.' "What?!?" he shrieked. "Judith Sheindlin, right? Isn't that the crazy judge you had all the stories about?"

"Oh my god," he said. "I can't believe it. Are you fucking kidding me? Her own show?" "Yeah," I laughed. "It's pretty entertaining, too. You should check it out." "Oh God," he groaned again. "I need another shot...."

I was pouring his shot when Danny Pope walked in with his wife Irene and a girl I hadn't seen before. She was tall and attractive and looked to be Chinese American. Both she and Irene were wearing light blue scrubs. The three of them came over and sat down at the bar. It appeared they'd already had a couple of drinks.

"Billy, this is my friend Christine," Irene said. "We work together at the nursing home." I extended my hand across the bar and was shaking Christine's hand when Irene added, "She's a virgin." I wasn't sure how I was supposed to react to that. I looked at Christine, smiled and said, "Nice to meet you." I looked at Irene and asked, "Why would you tell me that?"

Irene threw back her head and laughed. "Because she's 29 years old and she's a virgin! How many 29-year-old virgins do you know? Don't you think that's cool? I think it's really cool!" Still not sure how to respond, I said, "Well, yeah, I guess —" "Don't be embarrassed," Irene squealed, delighted at my discomfort. "Christine's really proud of it! Aren't you, Christine?"

Christine beamed, a big grin on her face. "You bet!" she said. "I'm not giving this away to just anybody! I'm saving it for the right guy." "Huh!" I said. "Well, good for you, I guess." I smiled at her and said, "I gotta say, I've got a lot of respect for you. I was abstinent for seven years back in the early eighties, and it was no picnic."

"Waddya mean, you were abstinent?" Irene asked. "I mean I didn't have sex for seven years," I answered. "Remember when

AIDS first started?" She nodded. "People were getting sick and dropping like flies," I said. "There wasn't any information in the beginning, nobody knew anything about it." Christine interjected, "I remember. They were calling it 'gay cancer,' because they didn't know where it came from or how you got it…"

"Exactly!" I said. "Well," I continued, "I figured the only way to make sure I didn't get it was to stop having sex. So I did." Danny had been listening quietly up to this point but now interjected. "Are you saying that you didn't have any sex for seven years?" "Yeah, dude, that's what I'm telling you." "No sex at all?" "Nothing at all. I was completely celibate." "Wow! Was it hard?"

"It wasn't hard for seven years!" Irene shrieked, swatting his arm. "Weren't you listening?" They all cackled while I rolled my eyes. "Well, seven years doesn't impress me," Danny said when he finished laughing. "I remember when I didn't have sex for thirteen years!" "What?!?" I exclaimed, "You didn't have sex for thirteen years?" "Thirteen years!" he repeated. "Wow. What happened?" "I turned fourteen," he chortled.

Shaking my head and laughing, I walked down to the other end of the bar and looked around. The place was heavy with regulars. In addition to Danny and Irene, the Bowery Boys were out in full force, as well as Black Lil, Buzzy, Fat Sara, Paco, and Miguel. My old friends Vicky and Liisa (yes, she spells it with two "i"s) from my waiter days at the Riviera Cafe and the South Street Seaport were there, as well as Edgar (without Amber).

I was pouring a beer and talking to Irene and Black Lil when suddenly, over all the other noise in the bar, I heard a familiar, rhythmic banging sound coming from the door to the Ladies'

Room. Alarmingly, it was the same sound I'd heard the night the girl had OD'd in there. Oh no, I thought, please don't let this be happening again! I looked toward the door and said, "Shit! What's going on in the Ladies' Room?" I stopped drawing the beer and went to grab the key. It wasn't there.

Irene started laughing, and said, "It's all right, Billy, that's just Christine!" "Christine!" I said. "What the hell is she doing?" "She's in there with Jackie Maddox," Irene replied. Jackie Maddox was one of the neighborhood 'Bowery Boys'. We listened as the banging persisted. Other people were beginning to take notice of it now as well. Irene looked at me. "He must be fucking her up against the door."

I shook my head in confusion. "What do you mean, 'fucking her'?" I asked. "I thought she was a virgin?" Irene laughed again. "She is a virgin," she said. "She told me that he fucks her in the ass." I stood with my mouth open, speechless. The same girl who proudly brags about "saving it for the right guy" has no problem taking it up the ass in a public bathroom. I had no words.

A few minutes after the banging stopped (the noise and the act), Christine and Jackie emerged from the bathroom. Jackie had the good grace to look sheepish as he broke away to go back to his friends. Christine walked over to the bar, returned the key to me with a sweet smile and said, "Thank you." I took it and hung it back up on its hook, shaking my head. Sometimes I just don't get it.

CHAPTER TWENTY-THREE

On that Monday night, October 30, I planned on closing quickly and going right home at the end of the evening. The next night, Halloween, was Characters' busiest night of the year. It was going to be a long and crazy shift, and I wanted to be rested and ready for it. The bar had been slow, and the night was almost over when my friend Richie showed up about 3:30.

Richie is a Luke Perry lookalike. He lives in Queens with his girlfriend and her mother and is an aspiring standup comic. In his act, he tells people he's Irish, Puerto Rican and Italian, and likes to get drunk and steal the hubcaps off his own Cadillac. Since I've known him, he's had at least a half dozen different jobs, including construction worker, rent-a-cop, and motorcycle mechanic. If he was Native American and joined the army, he'd be the Village People.

I gave last call soon after he got there, and since we hadn't seen each other in a while I told him to hang out so we could catch up. I'll ask people to hang out sometimes while I close out the register. We'll have a drink and shoot a couple of games of pool, but I always make sure we're gone by 5:30, when Jose comes in to clean. If Jose gets there earlier, or I lose track of the time and am still there when he shows up, he tells Sal.

Sal doesn't care. He knows I'm not selling liquor after closing (which would be illegal), just drinking it. And no laws are being broken if everyone on the premises after closing is an employee. But the people I ask to stay obviously don't work for the bar, so technically shouldn't be there. Not wanting to ruffle any feathers, I just make sure to be gone before Jose arrives.

That night after closing, we were halfway through our second game of pool when I asked Richie what he was doing for work these days. He told me he'd gotten a job servicing jukeboxes. "What?!" I said. "Are you serious?" "Yeah," he replied, "I go all over the five boroughs. It's not bad, they like me so they pretty much leave me alone to get things done." He chalked his cue and said, "I have this key that fits every jukebox in the city."

"Every jukebox?" I asked him as he took his shot. The eleven-ball dropped in the side pocket. "Yeah," he answered, "it opens everything, the front and back." He pointed toward the jukebox. "That whole front piece moves up and down on a hinge…" "Yeah, I've seen that," I said, dismissively. "That's how they change and load the records."

"Right," Richie replied, "and there's a panel in the back that lets me access the mechanics inside. Oh, and of course, the cash drawer." He chalked his cue as he eyed the table, looking for his next shot. "Your key opens that little cash drawer that comes out of the side?" I asked him. Walking past me, he bent over to line up a shot on the ten ball. It hit the corner of the pocket and spun away. He stood up and looked at me. "Yeah, I have the key to open that."

"And it works on any jukebox? It would work on this one?" I asked, indicating ours. "Yeah, sure," Richie answered. "Why? You want to dip into it?" I thought for a minute. That could be cool, but for all the moral failings I have, stealing isn't one of them. Then again, I thought, who would I be stealing from? Sonny Peanuts and the mob. I suppose that morally, I could rationalize that stealing from criminals wasn't really stealing, but I knew that wasn't true. I also knew how stupid taking that risk would be. Still, I was curious.

"I don't know about dipping into it," I said, "but yeah, I'd love to see if it works on this jukebox." "Oh, it'll work," he replied with confidence. "C'mon, I'll show you." He laid his pool cue down on the table and walked over to the jukebox. I put my cue down and followed him. He pulled a key ring out of his jacket pocket and inserted a key into the small drawer set in the side of the machine. He turned it, and with a click, the plastic box holding the cash popped out a few inches. Richie bent over and pulled it all the way out, showing it to me. "See that?" he said.

I took the drawer. It was a hard plastic box, the same dimensions as a dollar bill and over a foot long. Compressed into it was a stack of singles and fives filling the box almost to the top. It would be so easy, I thought, to just take some of it and no one would be the wiser. Or would they? "Wouldn't they know there was money missing?" I asked. "There has to be a way to figure out if the drawer is short."

"Well, sure, but I don't think a lot of that kind of diligence is done. These machines are impossible to get into without a key, so it doesn't even occur to most people that the money would be tampered with."

"Yeah, well with my luck, this would be the first time they checked, and I'd be busted. Just put it back, it's not worth the risk." Richie shrugged and smiled. "Okay, if that's what you want." He bent over to insert the drawer. He got it halfway in and it stopped. He pulled it out and tried again and the same thing happened. "What the fuck?" he muttered. Pulling the drawer out again, he inspected it to make sure he was putting it in correctly and nothing was stuck to the outside of the box. He tried to put it in a third time with the same result. The drawer stopped halfway in.

"What the fuck," I said. "What's the problem?" "I don't know," Richie said, jiggling the drawer. "It feels like something's blocking it from going all the way in." I felt the first prick of fear poking at me. I looked at the clock. It was 5:20. Jose would be here at any minute. If he showed up before we got the cash drawer back in we were busted. I was afraid that if he told Sal and Sal told Sonny, I could be looking at the inside of my own oil drum. "Can you see what's blocking it?" I asked.

"Not from here," he replied. "Let me go in from the back and see if I can figure it out." He pulled the jukebox away from the wall, angling it so he could get to the large black panel in the back. Using his keys, he unlocked the two locks holding the panel in place. He wiggled it and lifted it off, setting it aside.

"Here's the problem," he said. "Somebody put books in the empty space down here and now they're preventing the drawer from going all the way in." He fidgeted inside the panel's opening for a minute, then held something up for me. "Here, take this," he said. "Hold on, I've almost got it."

I looked down at what he'd handed me. It was a ledger. It was identical to the ones I'd seen downstairs on the shelf above the desk except for the binding. All the ones I'd seen downstairs had a green binding but the binding on this one was red. I opened it and fanned through the pages. It looked like what I imagine any ledger looks like, full of dates and columns of numbers that meant nothing to me.

Richie stood up and said, "There, I fixed it. The drawer's back in, I just had to move the books over to the right to make room. The panel's back on, and nobody will know we were in there." He stood up and began to push the jukebox back against the wall. "Wait!" I said, "You forgot to put this one in there," I said, holding out the ledger he'd given me.

At that moment, I heard the rattling sound of the exterior gate being pushed open. Shit! Jose was here! In about 30 seconds he was going to have the front door unlocked and would be walking in. I looked around frantically. My coat was sitting on a bar stool just a couple of feet away. I ran over and stashed the ledger under my coat just as the door opened and Jose entered.

"Hey, Jose," I called out. "Como esta?" Jose stopped just inside the door and looked at Richie, still standing next to the jukebox, the pool table, and me. "Hola," he said. "We were just leaving," I told him. "Sorry, I didn't realize how late it was. I don't want to get in your way, we're outta here."

Jose nodded, seemingly satisfied, and came into the bar. As he went toward the back storeroom, I caught Richie's eye and tilted my head toward the door. He nodded in acknowledgement and headed to the front door. I gathered up the ledger now wrapped in my coat and yelled, "So long, Jose, have a good day!" He poked his head around the side of the storeroom door and waved. "Okay, Senor Billy. Goodbye!" I left, confident in the knowledge that Sal would be hearing from Jose before the morning was over.

CHAPTER TWENTY-FOUR

When I first moved to the West Village in the mid-70s, Halloween was my favorite night of the year. The Village Halloween Parade was just a few years old at the time but had already become a hugely anticipated event. Since then, it's only gotten bigger.

The parade organizers gather the puppeteers and other key participants at 5 p.m. on Bank Street, all the way over by the Hudson River. At 6 o'clock, the parade begins, winding its way east toward 6th Avenue through the narrow streets of the West Village. As it progresses, hundreds of costumed revelers join the procession, and by the time the parade reaches the Jefferson Market Library on the corners of 6th Avenue and Tenth Street, its ranks are swelled to the point that marchers stretch from curb to curb.

The sidewalks on either side of 6th Avenue are so crowded they're virtually impassable. At the library, the parade turns left to go north on 6th Avenue up to 14th Street, where it takes a right turn to continue east. After one block on 14th St., the parade takes another right to head south down Fifth Avenue to its final destination, Washington Square Park.

And that's when the party really starts. The Washington Square Arch, lit from below by colored spotlights and festooned with giant spider webs, stands as a centerpiece to the festivities. Hanging skeletons bob up and down from tree limbs. Bands set up and play in three different locations in the park, and people in amazing costumes twirl, spin, and dance all around you. It's Mardi Gras in New Orleans, Carnivale in Rio and New Year's Eve all rolled into one.

When I was in my twenties, I loved it. Now that I'm in my forties, I hate it. At least I wouldn't have to deal with the usual crowds of people outside my front door blocking the street this year, because I was working. The parade's route takes it right past Characters. They knew from past years that it would be the busiest night of the year for the bar, so it was all hands on deck. Cormac, Diane, and I started at 4 o'clock and were all working the bar. Sal was there serving as bar back, restocking beer and liquor behind the bar for us as needed as the night went on. Mitzi and Paula (!) were doing general trouble shooting and crowd control at the door. Even Sonny Peanuts had been pressed into service, bussing tables, and taking out trash. Since we don't use any glassware on this night, bussing the tables consisted of carrying a trash bag around, emptying ashtrays, and clearing away the empty plastic cups and beer bottles people left lying around.

Everyone but Cormac and I had dressed in costume. Diane had on a ghost costume, and when she put the hood on I told her she looked like she was in the Klan. She took the hood off. Sal, Mitzi, and Sonny were all dressed in '70s garb. Mitzi and Sal looked like they were going for Sonny and Cher, while a bewigged Sonny seemed to be costumed as Tony Orlando. He had on a vintage brown leather jacket with enormous lapels, stitched with strips of leather. It looked familiar, like something I'd seen before, but I couldn't remember where.

"Whoa!" I said to him. "Awesome jacket! Where did you get that?" I asked. "My closet," he answered. "I've had it for thirty years." "You should see his closet," Mitzi said. "Sonny never throws anything out!" She laughed and punched his arm.

The night went pretty much as expected. The place was packed from 6 o'clock on. A lot of the regulars were there, joined tonight by a steady stream of partiers, most of whom were dressed in costumes. Cormac, Diane, and I worked at a frenetic pace keeping up with the demand for drinks, but everybody was pitching in and things ran smoothly. At about 8:00, Sal told me to take a break and took my place behind the bar.

When I came back, Old Man Eddie was squeezed in at the end of the bar. He had his wallet in one hand and was waving a cup in the other, trying to get Diane's attention. Seated next to where he was standing were a guy and a girl that seemed to be fighting. The guy wasn't in costume, but the girl was dressed as Nicole Brown Simpson. I wondered if she was a friend of Diane's. She was blonde and pretty and was wearing a football jersey with the number thirty-two and the name Simpson across the top. Her face was made up to look bruised and battered and a line of sticky looking fake blood ran across her throat.

It was tasteless but timely, and I loved it. It reminded me of the Halloween Parade back in 1978 right after "Mommie Dearest" came out. A big drag queen dressed as Joan Crawford marched the entire parade route repeatedly hitting a baby girl doll with an oversize wire hanger. She'd throw the doll down on the street and kick it before picking it up and beating on it again, screaming invectives the whole time. The crowd loved her.

This Nicole Simpson was no shrinking violet either. She was on a tear. Apparently, the guy she was with had felt the call of nature while they were out on the street, and he'd relieved himself in an alley against the side of a building. She was yelling at him so loudly I could hear her clearly above the rest of the considerable noise in the bar.

"You're disgusting!" she was railing. "Pissing on the street, you're fucking gross! The reason this city stinks in the summer is because of men! It's because of men like you, pissing on the sidewalks!" The guy finished chugging his beer. "That's not fair," he said, putting the bottle down on the bar. "It's not just men. It's dogs, too!"

I hung my head and shook it in despair. With guys like this defending us, our gender is doomed. 'Nicole' wasn't finished. "Men are so pathetic. You don't see a woman doing that! Women have the capacity to wait if they have to, but men are such fucking babies. You might be physically stronger," she said, getting in his face, "but everybody knows that women have a much higher tolerance for pain!"

I fantasized about putting her theory to the test right now. Old Man Eddie had heard enough. He turned and slurred loudly, "What the hell is this broad talking about?" He turned to her. "Men can put up with pain way better than any fuckin' broad!" She looked at Eddie. "Oh, really?" she sneered. "Have you ever given birth?"

Eddie's eyes narrowed. "Have ya ever been kicked in the balls, sweetheart?" he shot back. Momentarily struck silent, she quickly recovered. "Fuck off, old man," she said. "Up yours," Eddie replied. Sometimes the level of discourse at the bar makes me think I'm at the Algonquin Round Table. Eddie turned his attention back to the bar. "Diane!" he yelled. "Give me another goddam martini!"

Diane and I had been watching the whole exchange and now I turned so my back was to Eddie. "Have you been serving him martinis?" I asked Diane. I thought Diane knew that serving Eddie hard liquor always led to trouble. As long as he stuck to beer he could drink all day long, but as soon as he started on martinis, all bets were off.

"Not me," Diane answered. "I know better. I think Cormac might have made him one, and then Sal served him, too." "Great," I said. "Let's try to nip this in the bud and get him out of here before he gets in trouble."

"I'll handle it," Diane told me. She walked past me to the end of the bar where Eddie stood. I had my back to them and was making drinks when I heard Eddie yell, "Waddya talking about! I'm fine, I just want a fucking drink!"

I turned around to see Diane leaning into him and talking quietly. But Eddie was in full blown gin mode and ready for a fight. I saw Sonny Peanuts start to move in their direction, drawn by the sound of Eddie's yelling and turned back to my customers.

"You think you know more than me?" I heard Eddie yell at Diane. "I know what I can drink. I've been alive a lot longer than you have, sweetheart, and I know a lot more than you think I do. Ya wanna see how much I know? You wanna see how old I am? Look at my license!"

I heard a loud gasp and a crash and spun around to see a pale, shaken Diane leaning against the counter behind the bar. At her feet were three once full beer bottles, now broken and spilling their contents on the floor. I crossed over to her, reaching her just as Sonny Peanuts came up on Eddie. He took him by the arm and gently started to pull him away from the bar.

"C'mon, Eddie," he said, "You've had enough. I think it's time to go home." "Get your hands off me," Eddie yelled, shaking his arm. "Ya wanna grab somebody, go play grab ass with Sal's wife, you sonuvabitch!" Sonny dropped Eddie's arm in surprise and stared at him. Eddie continued yelling. "Ya think nobody knows about you and Mitzi? I know about everything! You bastards —"

"Okay, that's enough!" Sonny grabbed Eddie roughly and started to push him through the crowd toward the front door. The wind seemed to go out of Eddie's sails, and he stopped struggling.

I grabbed Eddie's jacket from behind the ice machine where he always stashed it and came out from behind the bar. "Sonny, wait!" I yelled, "Let me give him his jacket." Sonny paused and turned, waiting until I caught up to them. "It's okay, " I said to Sonny, "I'll walk him out." Sonny gave one more look at Eddie and growled, "You better watch yourself." Then he walked away. I handed Eddie his jacket and said, "Are you gonna be able to get home okay?"

Eddie was looking over my shoulder, past me. "Give me your hand," he said. "What?" I said.

Keeping his voice low he said, "Give me your goddamn hand like we're shaking." I put my hand out and he grasped it. I felt him pressing something that felt like a credit card into my palm. "Don't look down, just put this in your pocket. Don't let them see you do it." "Who are you talking about?" I asked him. "Just do what I say! People are watching," he whispered urgently.

I extracted my hand from his and palming the card, slipped it into my back pocket. We walked to the door and I watched as Eddie struggled into his jacket. He turned left toward 14th Street and disappeared into the crowd. I turned around and saw Cormac working all by himself and looking a little overwhelmed. I hustled back behind the bar and started filling orders. "Where's Diane?" I asked him.

"Sal told her to take a break, and then he disappeared too. When she comes back I'm going to take my break, if that's okay..." "Yeah, sure, dude," I said. "Of course."

Diane returned about twenty minutes later, and Sal came back to cover for Cormac while he was gone. We were in rhythm with each other, and things continued to run smoothly, despite the volume of business. Time passed quickly and before I knew it, it was after ten o'clock and I realized I hadn't seen Miguel all night.

I'd no sooner had the thought when he walked in the door. It took him awhile to work his way through the crowd, but eventually made his way down to the end of the bar where I was working. He asked for a beer and a glass of tequila. As I was pouring it I looked at him and said, "What's up, Mick? It's crazy out there, huh?"

"You have no idea," he said after downing half the tequila. "They made us get off the train at 18th St. because they said the 14th Street station was closed. I had to walk here from 18th, and the streets are packed with people. It took forever."

What a nightmare! I thought. "They closed the 14th Street station? What's up with that?" A girl sitting at the bar heard me and said, "I heard there was an accident. Somebody fell off the platform in front of a train." "Oh, Jeez," I said. "And what a night for it to happen." The girl's companion chimed in, saying, "I heard it's going to be two or three hours before they can reopen the station. I'm glad I live in the Village and don't need to get the train home."

"No shit," I concurred. Miguel called me over and slipped me a package. I told Diane and Cormac, "I'll be right back," and headed downstairs to do a line. When I came back up I returned to the bar and, fueled by the coke, worked like a dynamo. By then, the parade had been over for almost an hour. A lot of the crowd on the sidewalks had dispersed, with most of them headed over to Washington Square Park.

At about 2 o'clock some more drama played out when Sal and Mitzi started arguing about something. They took the 'discussion' downstairs before I could hear what it was about, but after only a few minutes Mitzi reemerged from the basement and stormed out. Sonny, who'd been hanging by the pinball machine inside the front door, followed her out a few minutes later, and I thought back to what Old Man Eddie had said earlier about the two of them. Interesting....

As soon as Mitzi and Sonny left, Fat Sara slid off her barstool and went downstairs to see Sal. They didn't emerge from the basement until the end of the night. The bar stayed busy right up until closing, but we managed to get out fairly quickly when the shift ended. The usual lot of late-night lingerers weren't around, probably because even though it was Halloween, it was still a weekday and a lot of people had to work the next day. It had been a long shift, but I made a lot of money and was just glad it was over.

Walking in my front door shortly before five, I was exhausted and looking forward to taking a long, hot shower and falling into bed. I took my pants off, and as I folded them, something fell out of the back pocket and hit the floor. Oh, I remembered, it's that credit card Eddie gave me to hold. I bent down to pick it up. When I looked at it, all thoughts of sleep flew out of my head. It wasn't a credit card at all, it was a license. Samantha Bigelow's license.

CHAPTER TWENTY-FIVE

I didn't sleep well that night. Since finding Samantha's license in my pocket my mind had been racing. What the hell was Old Man Eddie doing with the murdered woman's license? And what had he meant when he slipped it to me and said people were watching? What people? What did Eddie know?

I finally got up and showered just before noon, knowing I wasn't going to get any more sleep. I needed to go to the bar and talk to Eddie. I didn't know what kind of a game he was playing, but I was pretty sure it was a dangerous one. Unfortunately, when I got to the bar Eddie wasn't there.

I decided to go back home and come down again later to see if he showed up. On the way, I picked up the Post and stopped by Joe Jr's. to grab a burger to take home. Louie, the regular counterman, was behind the register, and I gave him my order. I watched as he threw my burger on the grill, then headed to the men's room at the back of the coffee shop.

As I emerged from the bathroom a few minutes later I passed the last booth against the wall. Sitting by himself with his back to the door and wearing a baseball hat pulled low, was Ronaldo Sagarro. I noted absently that he'd shaved off the mustache I'd found so unflattering.

I was going to pretend I didn't see him and walk right by, but I was too slow. That moment it took me to recognize him was long enough for him to look up and see me. We made eye contact, and I said, "Hey, Ronaldo, how ya doing?" He put his right hand out for me to shake. I took it, and he said, "Hi, Billy. I'm okay."

"You shaved your mustache," I observed. His left hand went to his mouth. "What? Oh, yeah," he said. "Just this afternoon." He took his hand away from his mouth and looked at me. "I'm sure you know what's going on with me, huh?"

Oh, God, I thought, could this be any more awkward? He was still holding my hand for crissake. "You mean that stuff that was in the Post?" I asked him. "Yeah, I saw that, man, I'm sorry." He released my hand. "What's going on with that? How are you holding up?" He looked away from me. "I'm holding up great for somebody who's about to lose everything." "But you haven't done anything wrong, right?"

He laughed and looked at me. "Do you really think that matters at this point? It's all about perceptions and appearances. By the time they determine I haven't done anything criminal it's already too late. The damage has been done. Hell, it's already done. I'm finished. All because of a bottom feeding muckraker with nothing better to do than screw up people's lives. A person like that deserves to be dead."

"So, you know about what happened to her," I said. He snorted. "What do you think?" he said. "Now they're even looking at me for that. They've had me in twice already for interviews and they can't verify my alibi, so my life's a friggin' nightmare. What's left of my life, I should say."

"What's the problem with your alibi?" "Probably the fact that I don't have one. I caught that bug that's been going around and was in bed for two days. I had the phone unplugged and didn't see or talk to anybody. Jesus, if I was going to kill somebody, I would have at least tried to cover myself better than that."

Unless you didn't plan on killing her and it just happened, I thought. Too bad the 'bug' can't testify. It could clear both Ronaldo and Miguel. I was rescued from having to prolong the awkward encounter when Louie called to me from the front of the diner. "Billy! Your food's ready!" I put my hand out to Ronaldo. "Listen, man, if you can think of any way I can help you out, please let me know. I'm really sorry for what you're going through..."

He took my hand and shook it. "Thanks, Billy." He gave me a sad little smile and said, "I've known you a lot of years. You've always been a decent guy, and I appreciate that. You take care." I walked up to the register and collected my food. I paid and left Louie a big tip before exiting. I never felt like a bigger piece of shit in my life.

CHAPTER TWENTY-SIX

When I got upstairs, I put the food from Joe Jr's in the refrigerator. My conversation with Ronaldo had killed my appetite. Settling on the couch in front of the television, I sat back and picked up the Post. I found a story about last night's incident at the subway station on page three. There wasn't much information. It reported that a little before nine o'clock last night, a man was jostled or fell off the crowded subway platform and fell in front of the train as it was entering the 14th St. station. According to the article, no wallet or identification was found on the victim. The station was closed for over three hours, it said, resulting in myriad problems for the Halloween Parade revelers trying to get home from the Village.

At 4 o'clock I returned to Characters to find that Eddie had been a no-show all day. I kept thinking about the subway accident, and I didn't have a good feeling about it. The accident happened shortly after Eddie left the bar, but I was still holding out hope it wasn't connected to him. The paper said the victim had no wallet on him, and I distinctly remembered Eddie waving his wallet at the bar. Still, the timing was too coincidental for me to rule out the possibility of it being Eddie…

Eddie hadn't shown up all day, and Eddie always showed up. In all the time I'd been coming to and working at Characters, I couldn't remember a single day when he'd stayed away. And I couldn't get the driver's license he'd slipped to me out of my mind. I decided I'd better check on him.

* * * * * *

I'd been to Eddie's apartment once before. He'd taken a fall one night leaving the bar and Fat Sara and I insisted on accompanying him home in a cab to make sure he got there safely. Fortunately, I remembered the building on 23rd Street. When I saw it, I told the cab driver to pull over in front.

I exited the cab and stood on the sidewalk looking up at Eddie's building. As I started up the front stairs, a kid I judged to be about twelve or thirteen ran past me and opened the front door. He held the door for me and I nodded my thanks and stepped into the foyer, scanning the mailboxes quickly. I saw E. O'Brian written on the box for apartment 1C. The kid had unlocked the interior door by now and I followed him into the building. He glanced over his shoulder at me as he headed up the stairs and I proceeded straight ahead down the hallway, assuming 1C would be at the back of the building.

I reached the door to apartment 1C and knocked. Listening intently, I strained to hear anything from inside but there was only silence. I had a sick feeling growing in the pit of my stomach that the apartment's resident was in the City Morgue, wearing a toe tag. But I could be wrong. Eddie could be inside, injured, or lying sick, and maybe didn't hear me.

I reached up to knock again more forcefully. This time, when I hit the door, it opened, and I realized it hadn't been shut properly. Lowering my arm, I pushed it open carefully and peered around the side. As soon as I did, I knew my fears were justified. I was too late.

I quickly entered the apartment and shut the door behind me. I stepped into a scene of complete devastation. There were papers strewn everywhere. A desk sitting under a window had had all its drawers pulled out and emptied. The cushions on the furniture had been cut open and the stuffing was everywhere. Chairs and tables had been overturned and a closet near the front door had been emptied of all its contents. They were strewn all over the floor, covered in the dirt from a vacuum cleaner bag that had been emptied over them. Even the back of the television had been broken open.

A quick walk-thru of the apartment confirmed what I already knew. The entire place had been ransacked and trashed, and there was no sign of Old Man Eddie anywhere. Whoever conducted the search had done a thorough job. Every room had been taken apart. Whatever the searcher thought was here was something he wanted very badly.

I had looked in the living room, bathroom, and bedroom before ending up in the kitchen. As I looked around at the complete destruction, I shook my head. Cannisters had been emptied and the door had been broken off the oven. The refrigerator door stood open, and all of its contents emptied onto the floor. Ironically, it looked like the only thing left undisturbed was the trash can, which still stood upright next to the stove.

I turned to leave when I was struck with a thought. Could it be that simple? I remembered Eddie telling me the story of where he'd found the mysterious package originally. It would be just like him to hide it where I now thought it might be. I crossed the kitchen in two steps to the trash can. I grabbed it and turned it upside down, emptying the contents from the bag onto the floor. I squatted down and sorted through it but didn't see anything like the duct taped white garbage bag Eddie had described.

Disappointed, I lifted the trash can to put it back next to the stove. When I hefted it though, it felt like there was still something inside. I looked into it, but the bag was empty, I had dumped everything. I put the trash can down and unfastened the now empty bag from the top edges. I pulled it out, and there, underneath it and sitting on the bottom of the can, I saw it. It was just as Eddie had described it, a white plastic garbage bag with duct tape wrapped around it.

I reached down and pulled it out of the trash can. I turned it over in my hands, wondering what was inside that was so valuable to someone. It had some heft to it, and I could make out the shape of a notebook and feel papers inside it as well. I realized my hands were shaking, and knew I needed to get out of there as fast as I could. I'd take this home and open it there. Maybe then I'd have some clue about what the hell was going on. I put the package inside my jacket and let myself out.

I was going down the front steps when I ran into the kid who'd let me in. "Were you here to see Eddie?" he asked when he saw me. His question took me by surprise. "Why?" I asked. "Have you seen him?" "No," he answered. "I just wondered. You're the second guy today who's come looking for him. I thought it was funny 'cause nobody ever visits Eddie, and now two people in one day..."

"Who else was looking for him?" I asked. "Some guy with a mustache was here real early this morning. Said Eddie was expecting him but he wasn't answering his bell, so I let him in the front door." This kid's parents have some serious work to do, I thought. He's a security nightmare for his entire building.

"Yeah, well, Eddie's a popular guy these days," I said. "If you see him, tell him Johnny dropped by." No way was I going to let this little blabbermouth know my real name. I didn't know who he might talk to. Before he could ask me anything else I hurried down the steps and headed home.

CHAPTER TWENTY-SEVEN

I was no further along with figuring out anything. I knew the mysterious "man with the mustache" was somehow involved, but I had no idea how, or who he was. Maybe the contents of the bag would give me some answers.

When I got home, I went into the living room and put the bag on the coffee table. It looked like the duct tape had already been cut through once and the bag retaped. Leaving the bag on the table, I headed into the kitchen to get a pair of scissors and retrieve a pair of rubber gloves from under the kitchen sink.

Returning to the living room, I put the gloves on. I cut the tape from the bag and unwrapped it before carefully emptying its contents onto the table. I pulled out a pocket notebook full of names and phone numbers. There was also a wallet, a couple of larger notebooks, a lot of loose papers, and an old copy of the West Side News.

At the very bottom, underneath it all, was the hefty object I'd felt. It measured about eight inches by eight inches and had some solid weight to it. It was double wrapped in a bar rag. Resting it on the table I unfolded the cloth from the four sides, revealing a heavy glass ashtray. It was covered in dried blood.

I knew I was looking at the weapon used in Samantha's killing. Any doubt of that was erased by what was in the wallet. There was no license, which was no surprise since Eddie had given it to me, but three different credit cards and a library card bearing her name confirmed the wallet belonged to Samantha Bigelow.

I picked up the notebook with the phone numbers and fanned through it, then picked up one of the large notebooks, I opened it and found the pages filled with what I thought were scribblings, but then recognized as Gregg's shorthand, the kind secretaries use when they take dictation. Who the fuck writes in shorthand, I thought? I put it down and picked up the copy of the West Side News. It was the same issue from October 4 that Miguel had shown me at the bar. I opened it to the page with Samantha's column and sat staring at it. Samantha had signed her autograph at the top of the column, right across the picture of her face. It was personalized "To Rosalita...."

What the hell was this? Of course, I knew what it was, as surely as I knew the first name of Miguel's mother was Rosalita. But Miguel told me he hadn't seen Samantha on the Friday she was killed. That was the day he was supposedly laid up with the bug that had been going around. I'd talked to him on the Wednesday night before her murder. Was it possible that he'd maybe seen her on Thursday? If so, then why hadn't he told me that when I asked him?

I put everything but the pocket notebook back in the bag and looked around for somewhere to stash it. In the end, I decided to put it in the same drawer in the living room credenza where I'd put the ledger from the jukebox.

Sitting back down on the couch, I picked up the pocket notebook and thumbed through it. I saw that Samantha had written "VV" at the top of one of the pages. Under the heading were four numbers. All but one of them had a line drawn through it.

Assuming 'VV' was an abbreviation for Village Voice, I called the one name that hadn't been crossed out, Sol Topp. It rang only once before it was picked up. I could hear Nirvana blasting in the background before a deep, bass voice said, "Sol Topp." "Mr. Topp," I said, "My name is Billy Collins...." "How did you get this number?" he interrupted. "I - I got it from Samantha Bigelow," I stammered.

Suddenly the music in the background cut off, and I could hear him readjusting the receiver against his ear. "Who is this again?" he said. "My name is Billy Collins. You don't know me, and I'm not even sure you're the person I'm looking for. Can I ask you, did you have an appointment to meet with Samantha Bigelow last Friday?"

There was a long pause before he answered. "Yes, as a matter of fact I did. Might I ask how you knew this?" "I was working for Samantha. I found your number in her address book and was wondering if I could meet with you." "Why?" he asked. "What's this about?"

"I'd rather not say over the phone. It's important, though, or I wouldn't be bothering you." I paused, waiting for a response but the line stayed silent. "It's about her murder," I said. The silence stretched on for so long I wondered if we'd been disconnected. Then he said, "Where do you want to meet?" I thought fast and asked, "Do you know French Roast on 11th and 6th?" "The coffee place? Yes, I know it. What time can you be there?"

Since it was only a block away, I could be there in five minutes. "You tell me," I said. "How's twenty minutes from now? Can you do that?" "That's fine," I replied. "I'll meet you in the back room, up the stairs. "I'm short with brown hair and I'll be wearing jeans and a black leather jacket." "I'll see you in twenty," he said and disconnected.

Twenty minutes later, I looked up from my coffee and saw a large, bald man approaching me, carrying a cup of coffee, and balancing two pastries on a paper plate. Appearing to be in his fifties, he stood about 6'1', probably weighed 250 pounds and was wearing black framed eyeglasses. He was dressed in a rumpled sport jacket and pair of wrinkled slacks, both of which looked like he'd slept in them. In what I assumed was a concession to the crisp weather outside, he had a woolen scarf wrapped around his neck and was wearing brown leather gloves.

"Billy?" he asked. When I nodded, he put the coffee down and carefully lowered the plate of pastries to the table. Unwrapping the scarf from around his neck, he laid it over the back of the chair before beginning to remove his gloves. "Why don't you leave those on for now?" I suggested. He raised his eyebrows as I told him, "You'll see why in a minute."

Still looking at me quizzically, he pulled out the chair across from me and slowly lowered himself into it. His tie was loosened around his unbuttoned open collar, and I probably could have told you what he'd had for breakfast and lunch from the stains on the front of his shirt. Undoing the button on his sport jacket, he wiggled around in the chair, adjusting his bulk. Once settled in, he took a large slurp from his coffee. After dabbing his mouth with a napkin, he placed his hands palms down on the table, leaned back, and fixed me with a stare. "So what's this all about?" he said.

I'd been thinking about the best way to go about this. As Sol Topp leaned over to take a big bite out of one of his pastries, I pulled the bag that I'd taken from Old Man Eddie's out from under my chair and put it on the table. I'd added the ledger from the jukebox into the bag as well, but I'd removed the bloody ashtray and left it at home in the credenza. The pocket notebook was in my fanny pack. "These are Samantha's notebooks and papers," I said. "I know she was working on something big, and I wondered if you know what it was."

Putting the pastry down and sliding his plate over, he reached across the table to open the bag and look inside. "Where did you get these?" he asked. "That's not important right now," I said. I gently extricated the bag from him and rested my hands on top of it. "I need to find out what the story was Samantha was following, and if it had anything to do with what happened to her."

I'd been debating with myself how much I was going to reveal to Sol Topp and thought that maybe the best way to learn anything from him was to play it straight. Plus, I was in over my head, and I knew it. I needed somebody I could talk everything through with. As I talked, he listened, while eating his pastries and sipping his coffee. I started at the beginning, telling him about Characters and my first meeting with Samantha, and finished up telling him about the package I'd found at Eddie's.

I didn't tell him about the ledger we'd found in the jukebox, nor did I mention finding the ashtray that had been used on Samantha. When I was done, I sat back and took a breath. He sat in silence, having finished both his coffee and his pastries, looking at the bag sitting on the table between us. Then he shook his head and exhaled loudly.

"So can you help me?" I asked. "Do you know anything about what this big story was that she was working on?" He sat and looked at me for a long time. I figured he was weighing what, if anything, he was going to tell me, Finally, he seemed to come to a decision. Clearing his throat, he looked around before looking back at me and said, "Money laundering."

"Money laundering?" That was completely unexpected. But wait... I reached in the bag and pulled out the ledger from the jukebox and handed it to him. As he thumbed through it I told him the story of how it came to be in my possession.

"Well!" he exclaimed, shaking his head again as he went through the pages. When he finished, he closed the book and set it on the table between us. He sat staring at it, not saying anything for the longest time. Finally, he said, "Okay, I guess it's my turn now...

He cleared his throat again and began. "Samantha called me about three weeks ago. I'd sent her a note congratulating her on the success of her new column, and she contacted me when she got it. She thanked me for the note, and told me that the column was small potatoes compared to the story she was developing, and suggested it was something I might be interested in." I sat silently, listening to him.

"Samantha always played it pretty close to the vest when she was developing a new story," he continued. "I used to work with her a lot back in the day, and I know how she operates...well, how she operated, I guess I should say. She was definitely on to something, but wasn't ready to share anything yet, other than it concerned a money laundering operation." He nodded toward the bag. "Have you looked through any of that yet? There might be something there that could tell you what you're looking for."

"That's the problem," I told him. "I didn't know what I was looking for. And even if I did, everything in the notebooks is written in shorthand." I looked at him and he raised his eyebrows. "You don't happen to know shorthand, I suppose," I said. "Actually," he replied, "I do." Indicating the bag, I asked, "Would you like to go through this and see if any of it means anything to you?" "I'd love to," he replied, "but maybe we should think about turning it all over to the police. If this stuff came from her apartment, you're in possession of evidence from a crime scene."

"Well, we don't know for sure where it came from, do we?" I argued. "Old Man Eddie pulled it out of the trash at Characters, and we don't know where it was before that." Of course, I knew it was from the crime scene, the presence of the ashtray confirmed that. But Sol Topp doesn't know about the ashtray, and I wasn't ready to reveal that information to him yet. I was still thinking about money laundering, and how that might be connected to the bar.

"Could Sal and Paula be using the bar to launder money?" I asked him. I thought back to that afternoon in the basement when I found Paula looking through the ledger, and just couldn't picture her being involved in something like that. But Paula doesn't handle the accounting for the bar, I remembered, Sal's wife Mitzi does. I told Sol Topp this and then wondered aloud, "Are Sal and

Mitzi laundering money? How would that even work? And if they are, does Paula even know about it?"

If Sal and Mitzi were laundering money, I was even more reluctant to go to the police, because, frankly, I didn't trust them. There was a reason Rudy Giuliani wasn't involving local precincts in his drug raids. There were too many leaks, and the risk of someone being on the take was very real. I could be exposing myself to greater danger if I got the local precinct involved.

Sol put a hand up to rub his fleshy jaw and straightened up in his chair. "I still think you have to turn all of this over to the police. There's a possibility it could be relevant to their investigation."

"Listen," I proposed, "how about you take all this stuff with you and go through it? If there's nothing important or relevant, then there's no harm, no foul. If you do find something you think the police should know about or would help their investigation, then turn it over to them." I pushed the bag across the table to him. "I suggest you get a pair of latex gloves to wear before you handle any of this." He nodded his head and pulled the bag in front of him. Twisting in his chair to reach behind himself, he retrieved his scarf and started to wrap it around his throat.

"One more thing," I began as he started to rise out of his chair. "If you do decide to turn it over to the police, you have to promise to give me a heads up first — and to leave me out of it." I didn't add that I didn't want the bag in my apartment after I'd seen what they'd done to Old Man Eddie's place.

He pushed his glasses up with his middle finger and ran his hand absently across his chin. Finally, he looked at me and said, "Okay, let me take a look and see what I find. I told you I know shorthand, so the notebooks won't be a problem. Give me your phone number and I'll call you as soon as I've had a chance to go through everything. We can meet up and maybe have something to go on by then."

I wrote down my home phone number and the bar number as well and gave it to him. He stood up and looked down at me. "I suppose I don't need to tell you to watch your back. I'm not sure what you've gotten involved in here. If the people Samantha was investigating are the ones responsible for what happened to her, you sure as hell don't want them finding out about you." He picked up the bag. "I'll be in touch," he said, and walked away.

After Sol Topp left I went home. Tomorrow was the day I'd promised Teddy Pope I'd visit him at Riker's Island, and I had to be at the 59th St. Bridge at 7 a.m. to catch the visitors' transport bus. I knew I probably wouldn't get much, if any, sleep when I got home tonight and considered taking a nap, but I was too wired. I decided to run some errands in the neighborhood and grab something to eat before going into work, and that's what I did.

When I walked into the bar at eight o'clock, Diane was on the phone behind the bar. She waved me over. "It's Mitzi," she said, handing me the phone. Wondering what this was about, I took the receiver from her. "Mitzi?" I said. "It's Billy. What's up?" "Oh, Billy," she said, sounding flustered. "No, I didn't want to—" she stopped and then asked, "Is Sal there?"

I turned to Diane and said, "Diane, is Sal downstairs?" Diane shook her head and said, "No, I haven't seen him." "He's not here, Mitzi," I said. "I just got here myself, but Diane —" "Okay, thanks," she interrupted, and the line abruptly went dead. I pulled the receiver from my ear and looked at it. Well, nice speaking to you, too, I thought.

I looked at Diane. "Why did you hand the phone to me? She was looking for Sal." Diane shrugged her shoulders. "I didn't know that. She asked me if you were here." "Huh, that's weird." I said and hung up the phone. I forgot all about it almost immediately and got to work. The night passed uneventfully, and I was able to walk out the door at 4:15. As I headed home, I was thinking I might be able to catch a couple of hours of sleep before heading to Riker's after all. But that was not to be.

CHAPTER TWENTY-EIGHT

The first sign that my night was about to go sideways came when I stepped off the elevator outside my apartment. Approaching my door, I could see that it wasn't completely closed. I stood frozen on the landing, my keys in my hand, and felt my heartbeat accelerating. Crossing quietly to the door and pushing it open slowly, I flashed back to doing the same thing at Eddie's place just a little over twelve hours ago. When I entered the apartment, I thought of the famous Yogi Berra quote. It was deja vu all over again.

The place had been ransacked. It wasn't the total destruction I'd witnessed at Eddie's apartment, but I had a sinking feeling that that was because whoever had been there found what they wanted quickly. I walked down the hallway to the living room and my fears were confirmed. The drawers of the credenza had been pulled out, and their contents spilled all over the floor. I didn't have to look. I knew the ashtray that I'd left in the drawer would be missing.

I looked anyway of course, just to be sure, but it was gone. I tried to think of who could have done this. Anyone I knew from the bar would know I'd be at work all night and could take their time going through the apartment. But how had they figured out to target me, and was it the ashtray that they sought, or something else? Whoever did this had to be looking for either the bag I'd taken from Old Man Eddie's, or the ledger from the jukebox. If they found the ashtray, then they knew I found the bag Diane had hidden. Would they be back for the notebooks and papers?

I wasn't about to stick around to find out. I grabbed a backpack and threw some weed, rolling papers, toiletries, and clothes into it. I went to the hall closet and rummaged around through the clutter on its' floor until I found an old pair of boots sitting all the way in the back. Reaching down into the right boot, I pulled out a black bandana wrapped around a small, solid object. I placed the bandana on the floor and unfolded it. Inside was a small chrome- plated .22 caliber pistol.

I'd been given the pistol almost a year ago by my friend Tim Doherty. Tim was an exterminator, and Characters was one of the businesses he serviced. Once a month he came in to spray the place at the end of the night after everyone left. We became buddies, and since Characters was the last stop on his route, he got in the habit of hanging out with me when he finished work.

About a year ago he happened to walk in just in time to see Matty Payne, one of the neighborhood 'Bowery Boys,' pull a knife on me. Matty was drunk and coked up and was trying to shake me down for coke or money to go buy coke. I told Matty to put the knife away and go home. It was 4 o'clock in the morning, I said, and even if I gave him money, he wouldn't be able to get anything. I suggested he call it a night and told him that I'd hook him up tomorrow.

It was at that moment that Tim walked in. I don't know whether it was what I'd said or Tim's timely arrival, but Matty folded like an accordion. He put the knife away, mumbled an apology to me and retreated out the door. I went back to wrapping the bottles behind the bar with cellophane so Tim could spray.

"What the fuck did I just walk in on?" Tim asked me. ""Did that guy pull a knife on you?" "Yeah," I said. "He's one of the neighborhood idiots, Matty Payne. He came and knocked on the door after I'd locked it, and l let him in." I shook my head. "Stupid." I finished wrapping the last bottle. "He was fucked up, but I handled it." I turned and smiled. "I'm glad you showed up when you did, though. He obviously has nowhere to go and it would have been a pain in the ass to get rid of him. So thanks, man."

I could tell Tim was disturbed by what he'd seen, but he took my cue and dropped it. He went about his work and didn't bring it up again. So I was surprised when he showed up the next night at closing. He sat at the bar and had some beers while the place emptied out. When the last customer left, I locked the door and went to sit next to him.

"I brought you something," he said, and reached into his jacket pocket. "Here. This is for you." He pulled out a small silver gun. "It's a .22," he said. "It probably won't kill somebody unless you shoot them point blank in the head, but it will definitely stop them." He raised an eyebrow and gave me a look. "And it trumps a knife."

I went to pick it up and stopped. "Is it loaded?" I asked him. "Yeah, but the safety's on. Here, I'll show you." He took the gun and pointed to the safety. He showed me how to work it, and then how to eject and load the clip. I was intrigued and listened carefully. When he finished, he handed it to me. "So, this is a present. I got it from a friend when I started working this job, because of the hours. Now I want to give it to you."

I was hesitant. "I don't know, Tim, I've never been a gun guy. They kind of scare me. I think you shouldn't have it unless you're willing to use it, and I don't really see myself using it." He nodded and said, "I get that. But look at it this way. That crazy fuck last night pulled a knife on you and if things had gone differently, you were completely defenseless. I see the people that hang out here, Billy, and I know they don't play by the same rules you live by. Do you want to end up in a hospital or a morgue just because you're more civilized, more 'evolved' than they are?"

He made a valid point. It was something that had crossed my mind at times as well.

"You have to get down and deal with them on the same level they're on, Billy, or you're not gonna…" He paused, as if he didn't know how to finish the sentence.

"I'm not gonna…what?" I asked. "Come out on top? Survive? Where are you going with this?" "You can laugh," he said, "but I see what you deal with here. And after what I saw last night, I'd feel a lot better if you'd just take the gun. Please. Just for a little while, at least until you know for sure that that Matty Payne guy isn't going to be a problem." So, reluctantly, I took the gun.

I carried it in my fanny pack for about a week, and if I'm going to be honest, just knowing it was there made me feel invincible. I was fearless. Then one day on the way to grab some lunch, I saw Bernie Goetz coming out of Papa's Place.

Bernie Goetz was the infamous "Subway Vigilante." He became an urban legend/folk hero to a lot of New Yorkers in 1984 when he fought back against a gang of muggers on the subway, shooting all of them. He lived right around the corner, on 14th Street, and I'd seen him around the neighborhood frequently, but not recently. When I saw him coming from Papa's Place that day, I was suddenly reminded that even though he'd been acquitted of all the charges against him, he still ended up spending a year in jail, the mandatory sentence in New York for carrying an unlicensed firearm.

Seeing him was like a wakeup call, a great big alarm going off. I realized that if I ever ended up using the gun, no matter what the justification, the consequences would be dire. Carrying a gun in New York City was probably the stupidest thing I could do. I went home immediately and took the gun out of the fanny pack. I wrapped it in a bandana and put it in a boot at the back of my closet, where it's remained undisturbed ever since. Until now.

I transferred the gun from the boot into my fanny pack, next to Samantha's pocket notebook. I zipped it in and fastened the pack around my waist. Slinging my backpack over my shoulder, I looked around the apartment one more time, turned out the lights and left.

As I closed the door and locked it, I recognized the futility of the action. A locked door was obviously no deterrent to whomever it was who had been here. But if they wanted to get back in, I was going to make them work for it.

CHAPTER TWENTY-NINE

The Hotel Senton sits on 27th Street. between 6th Avenue and Broadway. I'd partied at the Senton one night after work with some customers from out of town who happened to be staying there. That's where I headed now.

I couldn't quite get a handle on the place. While it was in no danger of getting a five-star rating in any guide book (or even a mention, for that matter), the rooms were big, the bathrooms clean enough, and they ran 24-hour free porn on four different channels. Most importantly, it was cheap, and they didn't require a credit card or identification for you to check in. The clientele was questionable, and I suspected some of the rooms rented by the hour. But there was also a fair amount of legitimate tourists there as well, mostly Asian and European families, well dressed and carrying sets of matching luggage. I wondered how they came to end up at the Senton. Maybe they heard about the free porn.

I got out of the cab and entered the glass front doors. A short staircase led up to the lobby, an open space with a worn sofa sitting against the right-hand wall. Potted palms sat in planters around the room. Some floor ashtrays and two chairs on the left completed the decor.

Across the lobby, opposite the front door and staircase, was a waist high counter, topped with bullet proof glass rising to the ceiling. The L-shaped enclosure ran from the left wall of the room across three quarters of the lobby. Its right-hand side extended back to the rear wall, creating the hallway that led to the elevator.

I went to the desk and checked in. As luck would have it, I got the last vacancy. It was almost 5 a.m., so I paid cash for two nights. The desk clerk gave me the register to sign, and I wrote Max Steiner. For some reason, it was the first name that popped into my head. What the hell, I thought. I was always a fan of the scores he composed for the Bette Davis and Humphrey Bogart movies made by Warner Bros., and, I figured nobody here was likely to know the name.

The clerk took the book and briefly looked at my signature, then handed me the key to room 309. He indicated the hallway next to him and said, "Elevator's right down there, Mr. Steiner. When you get to the third floor just go through the door on your right."

I thanked him, took the key and headed down the hall. It opened into a little alcove, with the elevator on the left-hand side and a pay phone on the right. Attached to the wall on one side of the elevator hung an 11" x 14" black and white framed photograph of Katharine Hepburn. On the other side of the elevator, also attached to the wall, was a vending machine that dispensed condoms. I'd have to find out who did the interior design. The photo of Hepburn looked to be a head shot from about 1935, her "Alice Adams" period. I wondered if the foreign tourists thought

Hepburn stayed here when she was in town. Maybe she even used this very condom machine!

The elevator arrived and took me up to the third floor, where I stepped off into a mid-sized anteroom. A console table sat against the wall opposite the elevator with a large mirror hung over it. There was an easy chair on either side of the table, which held a fake potted plant and some brochures. Doors at each end of the room led to two separate wings of guest rooms.

My room, 309, was to the right according to the desk clerk. I turned in that direction, and a red sign attached to the wall read 'Rooms 305 to 310.' It had an arrow pointing to the door, a heavy metal affair with a circular porthole window. When I pushed through, I found myself in a hallway with five doors opening off of it. Four of the five doors had yellow police crime tape stretched across them. The fifth door was Room 309, my room. Great.

I unlocked the door and stepped inside. It was a large room, with a queen size bed centered against the back wall. I went over to the bathroom and turned on the light to look around. Satisfied there was no one lurking inside waiting to butcher me while I slept, I crossed to the closet and deposited the backpack and the fanny pack inside. Returning to the bed, I sat down. I turned on the television and started surfing with the remote, landing on a movie channel showing "The Desperado." Getting back up, I grabbed the weed and rolling papers from the backpack and rolled a joint. While I smoked it I pondered who was prettier, Antonio Banderas or Salma Hayek. In the end, I couldn't decide.

I started to run over everything in my head. I was pursuing the theory now that Sal and Mitzi were laundering money through the bar and Samantha had somehow found out. Maybe

Paula tipped her off, either on purpose or inadvertently. It had to be unknowingly, I reasoned, because why would Paula tell her? Somehow, I thought, Sal got wind of what Samantha was up to and took her notes and papers so there'd be nothing for the police to find that would tip them to her investigation.

Then, I figured, he wrapped the stuff up and told Diane to get rid of it. She buried it deep in the trash can behind the bar, which made sense to me. That garbage bag would join the hundred other bags in the back alley that would be picked up and buried forever in a landfill somewhere in New Jersey.

But did Diane know what was in the bag she was throwing away? I wondered what Sal told her. What did Diane know? I had over an hour before I'd have to leave to catch the transport bus to Riker's. I decided to jump in the shower. I kept the bathroom door open, and an ear peeled for any strange noises. When I finished, I dried myself off, debating whether or not to shave. After looking in the mirror, I decided it could wait.

I went around the room and turned off all the lights, keeping the TV on with the volume turned low. I set the alarm in case I happened to drift off to sleep and laid down on top of the bed. After a minute, I got up and retrieved the fanny pack from the closet. I took the gun out and placed it on the nightstand next to the bed, then lay awake plotting out a course of action. I knew that when I got back from visiting Teddy, I had to talk to Diane again. There were too many things I still had questions about, and Diane was at the center of all of them. Eventually, I couldn't keep my eyes open any longer and decided to close them for a minute. Worn out from the day's events and mentally exhausted, I fell into a restless asleep.

CHAPTER THIRTY

I almost missed the transport to Riker's Island, making it with just minutes to spare. Once I found a seat on the bus and settled in, the ride out wasn't unpleasant. Seeing the neighborhoods of Queens for the first time was entertaining, and something of a revelation to me.

We crossed the 59th St. Bridge out of Manhattan and, once on the other side, traveled through streets lined with apartments, stores, restaurants, and clubs. In some areas they were nestled under elevated train tracks that ran above the road. The landscape began to change as we progressed through more residential neighborhoods, passing through blocks of detached single-family dwellings. It reminded me of the neighborhoods and houses I'd seen under the closing credits of "All in the Family."

When we finally reached Riker's, the bus had to go across a causeway that ran from the mainland out to the island itself, which sits in the middle of the East River. The causeway was lined on both sides by a sixteen-foot-high chain link fence topped with razor wire. Beyond the fences, all around us, lay the icy, choppy waters of the river, with its treacherous currents and dangerous undertows. At either end of the causeway was a gate and a guard booth.

The bus pulled into a parking lot next to the main building. After telling us to disembark they led us to the front doors, where guards instructed us to form a line. On the sidewalk sat white metal receptacles with posted signs declaring "any and all contraband" should be discarded at this point, the last chance to do so before entering the building. "Once inside, visitors will be searched," the sign stated, and "anyone caught attempting to bring anything illegal in will be prosecuted to the full extent of the law." The thought of Teddy wanting me to smuggle coke in for him went through my head. Dodged that bullet, I thought.

A surly, overweight prison guard led me through the last of what seemed like a dozen different checkpoints before finally depositing me in the Visitors Area of the jail. It was an enormous open space, with cinderblock walls painted industrial green and ceilings that soared to at least thirty feet high. The only windows were placed high up in the walls, just beneath the ceiling. With its scattered tables and molded plastic chairs, it could almost be mistaken for an employee cafeteria, the kind you'd find in a mill or a factory. Except most cafeterias don't have bars and steel mesh covering their windows and armed guards scattered around the room,

A lot of the tables were already occupied, and I recognized a few of the women I'd seen on the bus, now sitting and talking to men in orange jumpsuits. The guard showed me to a table, and I pulled out the molded plastic chair from under it and sat down.

"Busy day?" I asked the guard as he hovered over me. His eyes briefly met mine. "Hmph!" he grunted. Hmph, I thought? What the fuck does that mean? I started to say something but stopped when I thought about what this guy's life must be like. I couldn't imagine coming to work every day in this hellhole. Maybe I should cut him some slack.

He told me they were bringing Teddy down from his cell and he'd be there shortly. After reminding me that no physical contact with the prisoner was allowed, he walked off and left me alone. An almost overpowering smell of disinfectant and bleach permeated the entire area and the high ceiling wreaked havoc on the acoustics. Voices and sounds bounced and echoed everywhere, creating a disconcerting wall of unrelenting white noise. The assault on the senses was overwhelming. I had to tamp down my rising anxiety and remind myself that I was only going to be there briefly, and then I could leave.

I looked up to see Teddy, wearing an orange jumpsuit, being led into the room by another guard. As they approached the table where I sat, I noticed that he was walking with a slow shuffling movement that I attributed to the plastic flip-flops he had on his feet. I glanced around the room and realized all the inmates were wearing them. I smiled as a fleeting, random thought popped into my head: It's hard to look threatening when you're wearing socks and flip-flops.

They got to the table and Teddy pulled out the chair on the other side and sat down. We nodded at each other and waited for the guard to move away before we spoke. "You made it," he said. "Yeah," I said, "just barely. I almost missed the bus." "How was the trip out here?" Teddy asked. "It was good," I told him. "Interesting. It's the first time I've ever been out of Manhattan since I moved here, can you believe it? In twenty years, I've never seen

Queens." Teddy gave a small laugh then asked, "What's going on at the bar?" "Hah," I exhaled. "What's not going on? Where do I start?"

At the beginning would be the logical place, so that's where I began. Teddy had been locked back up before all of this started, so he didn't know about any of the things that had happened. Just as I had with Sol Topp, I laid out the whole story, from my first meeting with Samantha to the ransacking of my apartment. This time I left nothing out.

When I finished, I said, "So right now, I'm trying to figure out how Samantha's murder might be tied to the money laundering, but I haven't got a fucking clue how to do that. I don't have proof of anything. I've got the ledger, but I don't know what good that does me…."

"You need the corresponding ledger," Teddy said. I stopped, puzzled. "What do you mean?" I asked. "The ledger you got out of the jukebox, the one with the red binding—it has a date on it, right? Showing the time period the entries cover?" I nodded. "Yeah. March 1995, I think."

"So, there should be a corresponding ledger with a green binding for the same month. You need to get that ledger. When you compare the two, you should have the proof you need, at least regarding the money laundering."

"Of course!" I said, hitting my forehead. "What an idiot I am. I should have thought of that right away." "You've got a bigger problem, though," Teddy continued. "What's that?" I asked. "You said you think that Sal and Mitzi are laundering the money, but I think you're wrong. You're theory's based on a faulty assumption…"

And then Teddy told me something, something I knew would require me to rethink everything I thought I'd figured out. It was the piece of the puzzle that I'd been missing, the piece that made all the others fall into place. I knew now what I had to do.

CHAPTER THIRTY-ONE

When the bus from Riker's dropped me off back on 59th St. in Manhattan later that afternoon, I grabbed a cab to return to the hotel. On the way, I had him stop at a deli so I could pick up some food. My plan was to not leave the room and just stay holed up there until Monday, when I was scheduled to work. Before I returned to the bar, though, I needed to get the lay of the land. Since I thought Diane might hold the key to a lot of my questions, talking to her would probably be the best course of action.

Having gotten almost no sleep the night before, I crashed early when I got back to the room and slept through the night. When I got up Sunday morning, I decided to call Diane, but before I did that, I had another call to make.

Pulling the pocket notebook from my fanny pack, I looked up Sol Topp's number. I headed downstairs to call him from the pay phone located in the hotel lobby, across from the elevator. Under Katharine Hepburn's watchful eye I dialed his number and listened to it ring. When he finally picked up, it sounded like he was eating.

"Mr. Topp," I said when he answered, "it's Billy Collins..." "Billy," he boomed. "Where the hell have you been? Wait a minute -" I heard him continue to chew then audibly swallow. He cleared his throat and came back on the line. "I've been trying to get in touch with you!"

"Why?" I asked. "Did you find something in the notebooks?" "Oh, I found something, all right. Samantha had the whole investigation laid out, names, financials, sources, the whole nine yards." "And it's about money laundering?"

"Her notes outline the whole operation, run by a guy named Salvatore Piscatelli. It's huge, way bigger than you can imagine, a citywide network, and that bar you work in, Characters? It's one of the bars involved."

Gee, tell me something I don't know. "So, what do we do now?" I asked. "Well, that's why I've been trying to reach you. I know I said we'd discuss it first, but after reading the notebooks I felt I had no choice but to turn them over to the police. I wanted to give you a heads up before I did it, but I couldn't find you anywhere."

"Yeah, I thought it was a good idea for me to disappear for a while." I told him about the break in. "Sorry, I should have let you know." "Oh, that's all right," he replied, "I'm just glad you're all right. When I couldn't get hold of you, it made me nervous. After reading Samantha's notes and seeing the people she was looking into, I feared for your safety. Where are you, by the way? Are you safe?"

"For the moment," I said. "Who did you speak to when you contacted the police?" "They shuffled me around, but I finally landed with the detective running Samantha's case. A Detective Eugene Rame."

Eddie Murphy's friend, I remembered. "Listen," I said, "we should probably get together. I have a few things I need to take care of first, though, so let me call you tonight or first thing in the morning. We'll set up a time and place to meet." "That sounds good. I've got a lot of questions for you. This is shaping up to be big, I'm excited. Samantha did an amazing job of documenting this stuff. I have to give it her, she still had it."

"I have to go," I said. "Thanks for the heads up, and I'll talk to you soon." I hung up and looked at Katharine Hepburn. Waddya think, Kate, I asked her. Are we going to get out of this intact? It was time to find out what Diane knew.

I called her at home. The phone rang for so long I was about to hang up and try her at the bar. Then she picked up "Hey," I said, "it's me." "Billy," she exclaimed, "where the hell are you? We've been trying to get in touch with you for two days!"

My antennae went up. "What's up?" I asked. "Did something happen?" "You wouldn't believe what's been going on," she replied excitedly. "The police know who killed Samantha. It's all over!" "Waddya mean, 'it's over'?" I said. "Who did it?" "You won't believe it," she said. "I'm still completely freaked out."

"Who did it?" I asked again. "Who killed her?" "It was Sal!" she answered. "Sal killed Samantha!" "Sal?!" What??? "Yes! The police had a search warrant for his and Mitzi's place. When they searched his house, they found a glass ashtray in his home office. They think it's what he used to kill Samantha. It had his fingerprints all over it! They're waiting for the lab results to see if the blood on it is a match with hers." How the hell did the ashtray get from my apartment to Sal's desk?

"So did they arrest him?" I asked. "No, they can't find him," she told me. "He's gone on the run. They've issued an arrest warrant though, so it's just going to be a matter of time before they get him." Red flags were going up everywhere.

"I'm running late" Diane said. "I have to get ready for work. Why don't you come to the bar tonight at 8 when I get off? Sonny and Paula will be there, and we'll fill you in on everything." "All right," I answered. "I'll see you then." I hung up and thought about what Diane had just told me. I had a hunch I wanted to check out, and I also needed to collect something before I met up with Sol Topp. Looking at my watch, I thought that if I hurried, I could get to Characters and be out of there before Diane showed up.

I jogged over to Broadway and flagged down a cab. I had him take me down Broadway to 13th Street, and then across to the corner of 6th Avenue, where I hopped out. Across the street, I could see the accordion gate was drawn across the door at the bar. Good. That meant Jose was gone, and Diane hadn't arrived yet.

I hurried across the street and approached the doorway. Taking my keys from my pocket, I unlocked the padlock on the gate and opened it just enough to squeeze through. Using a second key, I unlocked the front door. As I entered the bar, I reached behind me and pulled the gate shut so it would appear to be closed to anyone going by. I went in the bar and threw the lock on the door behind me. Moving quickly, I went to the basement door. I opened it, flipped the light switch on the wall and descended the stairs.

It only took a minute to walk to the back of the basement and confirm what I'd come to see. Turning around, I checked my watch again and detoured over to the desk, and the ledgers on the shelf above it. I scanned them and found the one for March of 1995. That matched the date on the one with a red binding I'd given Sol Topp. I took the March volume down to look at more closely. It was identical to the one from the jukebox, differing only in the color of the binding. The contents made no more sense to me than the other one had, but I noticed that it was formatted and laid out in exactly the same manner.

I put the ledger inside my jacket and zipped it up. My eye went to the gap in the volumes on the shelf where I had removed the book. Fearing it might draw attention, I went to push the remaining ledgers together, and in the process accidently knocked over the framed photo Paula had sitting on the shelf next to them. I picked it up to put back, and when glancing at it, raised my eyebrows in surprise. I studied the faded clipping, read the caption, and looked at the picture again.

I put the frame back on the shelf and made my way upstairs. Crossing to the front door, I unlocked and opened it, stepping into the alcove between the door and the gate. I locked the door behind me, then checked the street before opening the gate and stepping out onto the sidewalk. I refastened the padlock and quickly walked away. I was pretty sure I'd finally put the whole thing together. Now what was I going to do about it?

I went back to my apartment. It didn't appear that anyone had come back in my absence. I checked the answering machine and saw I had twelve missed calls. Most of them were from Sol Topp and Diane. After clearing the call history, I called Eddie Murphy. It was time for me to meet Detective Rame.

CHAPTER THIRTY-TWO"

Not only did I meet Eugene Rame, but I also ended up spending the entire afternoon with him at the 6th Precinct. Sol Topp and (at my request) Eddie Murphy joined us, along with detectives from Homicide, Vice, and two guys from the Organized Crime Unit. It was a long and grueling, but ultimately productive, afternoon. By the time I left the station almost six hours later, I was prepped and ready for my meeting with Diane, Paula, and Sonny.

That night, as eight o'clock approached, I walked into Characters. I waved at Cormac and from the corner of my eye saw Eddie Murphy and Gene Rame sitting halfway down the bar. I walked past them to the end without looking their way. Cormac met me with a Jack on the rocks in his hand and said, "Diane's downstairs with Paula and Sonny Peanuts. They said to tell you to come down when you showed up." I took a healthy swig of my drink and, still ignoring Eddie and Gene, walked to the basement door. "Thanks, Cormac," I said. "Hold down the fort." He smiled and gave me a wave as I started down the stairs.

I heard voices coming from the other side of the basement. I followed the sound around the stairway to the back and saw Paula, Diane and Sonny seated around Paula's desk. An open bottle of red wine sat between Diane and Paula. The Florida brochures I'd seen Paula looking through were now stacked in a neat pile on the corner of the desk. Sitting on top of them, acting like a paperweight, were the darts from upstairs. Paula must have confiscated them again. In spite of my nervousness, the sight of them made me smile.

Paula and Diane were each holding a glass of wine, and neither one looked like it was her first of the night. Sonny Peanuts sat to the side, his chair tilted onto its two back legs and his feet resting on the desk. He held a full bottle of Heineken in his hand, and I took note of at least four empties sitting on the floor around him.

Diane was facing in my direction and was the first to see me. "Hey, Billy," she said. Paula and Sonny had been talking, but both stopped and turned to me when I appeared. I noticed Paula looked like she'd been crying. "Hey," I said. I pulled a chair from against the wall and spun it around, so it was backwards. I straddled the seat and leaned my forearms on the chair's back. I looked from one to the other. "So. What the hell is going on?"

Sonny took a long pull on his beer. He lowered his feet from the desk to the floor and fixed me with an intense stare. "I don't need to tell you that anything said here tonight goes no further. Ever." He broke his stare and glanced over at Paula, then Diane. Paula seemed to sniffle, while Diane nodded. I took a drink from my glass. "No, you don't need to tell me." I responded. "I think we all know what's at stake here. So let's cut the crap and put everything on the table so we can sort this shit out and move on."

Sonny looked momentarily taken aback. He seemed to regroup and started again. "This whole thing wouldn't have happened if you hadn't started feeding Samantha those stories." That took me by surprise. Was this the way they were going to play it? I shot a look to Diane who avoided my eyes. "What are you talking about?" I asked Sonny.

"All those fucking stories about the bar and the coke. What the hell were you thinking? When Sal found out he went crazy." "Are you saying that Sal killed Samantha because of the stuff she was writing in her column?" This wasn't what I expected to hear. They really must think I'm that stupid, I thought. "How — how could that even happen?" I asked him.

"He got her address from Paula and went to see her." I looked at Paula and she turned away. "He didn't go to kill her, he was just going to reason with her," Sonny said. I've seen the way Sal 'reasons' with people in the past. It's pretty one-sided and not very reasonable. I looked at Paula again. She was clutching a Kleenex to her mouth and looking at the floor. I turned my gaze to Sonny. "So what happened?"

"He was all coked up and had been drinking. I guess things just got out of hand. Fucking Sal! He never had any self-control. He ended up beating her to death with the ashtray. Then he grabbed some stuff to make it look like a break-in and we met up and came back here. Sal told me what he'd done, and I told him to hide the bag of stuff he'd taken inside the garbage. It'd get thrown onto that big pile of garbage bags in the alley and the trash pickup was the next day. So he called Diane to come downstairs and gave her the bag."

Diane interrupted. "He didn't give me any explanation, just told me to take this bundle upstairs and to bury it deep in the trash can behind the bar." "And you didn't ask why?" I asked her. She shrugged. "Why would I? I really didn't think much of it, to tell you the truth. It's not like it's the strangest thing he ever asked me to do…" She had a point. Unexplainable and erratic behavior was kind of the norm with Sal. "And that's it?" I said. "What happened with the police? How did they get on to Sal?"

"The phone records were the tipoff," Sonny explained. "They knew that all the calls between the bar and Samantha would have been with Diane or Paula. But they saw the calls back and forth at night and they knew that Sal was here at night. Sal denied even knowing her, let alone talking to her on the phone. That made them suspicious, since they knew he had."

"Wait a minute," I interrupted. "How did they know that?" "Because that's what I told them," Diane volunteered. I hoped my face wasn't revealing the confusion I felt. At least now I knew why the police hadn't questioned me. But I didn't understand why Diane would cover for me, especially if it meant throwing Sal under the bus in the process. "So they got a search warrant based on that?"

"Well," said Sonny, "that and a couple of other things they turned up. They had a witness description that fit him as well, I understand." Ah, that would be Minnie, I thought, and the 'mustached man.' "And of course," Sonny continued, "once they found the ashtray, it cinched it. His fingerprints were all over it. And the fact that he disappeared, of course."

Of course. I had my own thoughts about that, but I wasn't ready to play my hand yet. I wondered how they were planning to explain how the ashtray got into Sal's desk, when whoever put it there had to have taken it from my house. That person would also have to have known where I'd gotten it from. Maybe I was supposed to believe Sal had broken into my apartment and retrieved it. "And what about Old Man Eddie?" I asked, looking back and forth between the three of them.

"Yeah, well, that was unfortunate, wasn't it?" Sonny said. "When Diane told us about Eddie showing her the license, Sal freaked. I didn't know what he was planning to do. Since the ashtray ended up in Sal's desk, I assume he went to Eddie's and got it back." He looked at me as if trying to gauge my response. I kept my face neutral and waited for him to continue. He didn't say anything.

I glanced over at Paula and Diane. Diane returned my look but stayed silent. Paula stared at the floor, still clutching the Kleenex that she worked nervously through her fingers. It was clear that this was the story they'd decided to go with. It was time to show my cards and see if I could shake something out of them.

"That's interesting," I said. "There's just a couple of things I don't get." "What's that?" Sonny asked, taking a final drink from his beer. He drained the bottle and put it down on the desk. Tilting his chair back, he looked at me expectantly with raised eyebrows.

Staring at him, I said, "Well, to begin with, Samantha wasn't beaten to death, she was strangled." I heard Diane gasp. Sonny lowered his chair so all four legs were on the floor again. "Yeah, so?" "So I don't think you're telling me the truth. I don't think Sal killed Samantha."

Paula had stopped fidgeting and was now looking at me for the first time since I'd gotten there. Sonny shifted in his seat and said, "Waddya talking about? If Sal didn't kill her, who did?" "I don't know. Why don't we ask Diane?" I looked at her. "Diane? You want to tell me what happened?" Diane had turned pale, and now her eyes darted nervously back and forth between Sonny and Paula. "I don't know anything, why are you asking me?" she asked defensively.

I decided to bluff. "Because when I talked to Samantha Friday morning, she told me she was expecting you. Old Man Eddie saw you leave the bar that morning at 11:30 and you didn't return until forty-five minutes later. Which just happens to fall right into the timeline of when they think Samantha was killed. You want to tell me where you were?"

I watched as the three of them looked back and forth at each other. I got the impression they were trying to communicate something but couldn't get a read on it. Diane, looking trapped, finally spoke. She turned to Paula and Sonny. "I'm going to tell him," she said. "It's better if he knows the truth."

Sonny started to say something, but Diane cut him off. She turned to me. "You're right," she said. "I did go to Samantha's that morning. I was going to ask her to stop writing about Characters, but she refused, and we fought. I picked up her ashtray and hit her and when she fell, she hit her head again. I thought I'd killed her and didn't know what to do." She stopped and took a ragged breath and I saw tears rising in her eyes.

"I was so scared. I ran and got out of there but didn't know where to go." "So what did you do?" I prompted. "I was only a block from Paula's, so I went there." At the sound of her name, Paula went very still. "I told Paula what had happened. She told me to get back to the bar, so I'd have an alibi, and said she'd have it taken care. She said she was going to call Sal, so I left." She looked at me. "Did you mean it when you said Samantha was strangled?"

"Yes," I responded. "Which means you didn't kill her." A look of confusion on her face, Diane turned to Paula. "If I didn't kill her, then it had to be Sal. When you sent him over there to clean up, he must have strangled her."

Paula just sat there with a strange look on her face. She stared at Sonny. Sonny, looking suddenly discomfited, shifted again in his chair, and said, "All right, fine, Sal strangled her." He leaned toward me. "So we didn't tell you about Diane's involvement. What's the difference? It doesn't change anything. Whether he beat her head in or strangled her, Sal still killed her."

I looked at Paula. "Is that true, Paula? Did Sal kill your friend Samantha? If Sal was the person you called, then I guess he must have. Is Sal the person you called, Paula?" Paula looked like a deer caught in the headlights, shaking her head and looking back and forth between me and Sonny. Diane, watching us, said, "Paula? What's he talking about?" "Diane," I asked, "did Paula say she was going to call Sal? Or did she say Salvatore?"

Diane looked at me, confused. "I don't know. What difference does it make?" Paula started to cry quietly. Diane got up and went to kneel in front of her, then looked at me. "What the hell are you talking about? Paula called Sal. Who else would she have called?"

I gave an exaggerated shrug. "Oh, I don't know. Maybe her partner?" "Her partner? Sal is her partner — was her partner!" I turned to Sonny. "Sonny? You have anything you want to tell her?" Sonny sat and glared at me. Diane looked over at him. "Sonny?" she asked uncertainly.

"Just out of curiosity," I said, addressing Sonny. "What's 'Sonny' short for?" Sonny sat back and fixed me with his stare. "You think you're pretty smart, don't you?" he sneered. I considered that. "No, not really," I answered. "Certainly not as smart as somebody smart enough to run a citywide money laundering operation — Salvatore."

Sonny pulled a gun from his jacket pocket and pointed it at me. "You got that right, you little shit," he said. "Too bad you're too smart for your own good." Diane gasped and stepped back toward the desk, while Paula screamed and said, "Sonny, no!" Diane was freaking out. She started to hyperventilate and said, "What the fuck is going on? Sonny, what are you doing? Billy, what's going on?"

"I'll tell you what's going on," I said, talking to Diane but keeping my eyes fixed on Sonny. "Sonny is Paula's partner, not Sal." I looked at Paula. "You wanted to retire, didn't you? But Sonny wouldn't let you. He and Mitzi were laundering too much money through here to give it up and he needed you to maintain the liquor license."

Sobbing, Paula spoke up haltingly. "When we opened, he told me I could retire when the license came up for renewal. But when the time came, he told me he'd changed his mind." "Shut up, Paula," Sonny said. Paula went on, her voice growing stronger. "He told me about the money laundering and said if I didn't renew the license, I'd get blamed for it! Mitzi had it all set up to look that way. I told Diane what they'd done."

"Shut up, Paula," he said again more forcefully, still looking at me. I turned to Diane. "That's when you contacted Samantha. You thought that if you could draw enough attention to the drug scene at the bar, it could result in a raid. The liquor commission would revoke Paula's license if the bar got raided, wouldn't they, Paula?" She looked down at the floor and nodded. I looked back to Diane.

"I guess you reasoned that Sonny couldn't hold Paula responsible for losing the license because of a drug raid. And once she couldn't be granted a license anymore, her usefulness to him would be over. She could retire, and the two of you could move to Florida. "You and Samantha decided to use me to tell her things that she could write up in your effort to get the bar closed. That was the endgame all along, wasn't it? To get the bar closed without repercussions to Paula?"

Diane dropped her head and said, "Yes, that was the plan." I looked at Sonny. "And when Paula called you for help that day, you realized you'd stumbled onto a perfect opportunity to take care of the Sal problem. What happened Sonny? Did Paula tell Sal about the money laundering?" My stab in the dark was confirmed by a muffled wail and renewed sobbing from Paula.

"Did he want to be cut in?" I continued. "Or maybe he was just gonna blow the whole thing up on you and his cheating wife," I said, fishing. "Sal was a fuck-up," Sonny snarled. "I loved him, but he was a fuck-up." "Yeah, you loved him. You loved him to death, didn't you? I've gotta say, the frame was pretty good, considering you were flying by the seat of your pants. You were making it up as you went along, right?" Sonny, who was glaring at me, now smirked.

"It was the Halloween costume that tipped me off," I told him. "You wore the same jacket you have on in the picture." I pointed to the framed clipping sitting on the shelf above the desk.

"The Tony Orlando wig and mustache was the big mistake. You were the 'mustached man' that Samantha's neighbor saw, not Sal. And you were also seen at Old Man Eddie's place wearing the same disguise. Once I found out that you were Paula's partner, the rest of it started to fit together. And of course, I knew all about you and Mitzi." I bluffed.

At the mention of Mitzi's name, Paula reacted. "That bitch!" she muttered into her tissue. Sonny shot her a look. I went on. "I figure that when Sal got back from prison, you and Mitzi needed something for him to do, so you hit on the idea of the bar. You'd put up the investment money but Paula was necessary to get the liquor license. Sal was gonna be the public 'face' of the place. He loved the idea of letting people think he was the owner, so the three of you told everyone that he was Paula's partner. It made him happy.

"I'm thinking you really did it to put one more layer of protection between you and the money laundering if things went wrong. With Mitzi ensconced as the accountant, and Paula's 'hands off' approach, I don't imagine it was hard to pull off." I looked at Paula. "I'm curious, Paula, did you know what they were doing?" Paula was weeping quietly into her tissue and shook her head.

I addressed Diane. "When Samantha tipped off Paula about what she'd discovered, Paula made the mistake of confronting Sonny. He probably denied it, so she turned to Sal for help." I looked at Sonny who just shrugged. I turned back to Diane. "Then when you thought you'd killed Samantha and ran to Paula, she called the man she'd known and partnered with for thirty years to clean up the mess. Salvatore Piscatelli."

"Oh, God," Paula groaned. "Shut the fuck up," Sonny snapped at her. I looked at Sonny. "When you got to Samantha's, she wasn't dead, though, was she? You knew that if she survived, your whole world would collapse. So you made sure she wouldn't survive."

Diane and Paula were now looking at Sonny. The look of fear and confusion that had been on their faces was replaced by something else. Sonny, sensing the change, rose out of his chair started to shout. "You're fucking crazy!" He looked at the women. "I never laid a fucking hand on her when I got there, she was already dead, I swear!"

Diane's face was deathly white, and she was shaking with rage. "You bastard!" she shouted. "You let us think that I'd killed her all this time!" Paula gave a piteous moan and said, "What have I done?"

I turned on her. "You let your murdering, lying partner kill one of your oldest friends, for money! And then you kept quiet while he blamed it on another friend." I looked back at Sonny. "A friend who's conveniently disappeared. What did you and Mitzi do to Sal, Sonny?" I pointed to the back of the basement. "For as long as I've worked here, there've been six oil drums down here. I counted them today, and guess what? Now there's only five. Is that what you did with him Sonny? Did you give Sal an East River funeral? Was he already dead when you pressed his fingerprints onto the ashtray?" Paula seemed to collapse within herself. "No, no," she moaned over and over.

Diane was beside herself. "You killed Sal, too? Oh my God, you're fucking crazy!" She grabbed the empty beer bottle off the desk and launched herself at him. He backhanded her, but she let the momentum of his blow carry her around. She spun like a shot-putter, bringing the hand holding the bottle up and around and smashed it across his face. It broke, shattering his tinted glasses.

Sonny screamed and threw his hands up. I jumped up out of my chair, cocked my leg back and kicked like I was going for the end zone. I kicked him as hard as I could, just below the knee. The steel toe of my Doc Martens connected with his leg and I heard the satisfying crack of bone, followed by Sonny's scream. He collapsed, landing on top of Paula. As he fell, his finger reflexively pulled the trigger of the gun.

The sound of the gun going off was deafening, and out of nowhere I felt like someone had hit me in the shoulder with a baseball bat. He'd shot me! The bullet knocked me to the floor and the ringing in my ears prevented me from hearing anything. I was completely disoriented. I looked up to see Sonny trying to take aim at me again. He pushed off of Paula, who sprawled across the desk. Sonny, his injured leg unable to support him, collapsed on the floor in front of her.

There was a bang from somewhere above as somebody slammed open the basement door, followed by the sound of pounding feet coming down the stairs. I saw Sonny raising the pistol in his shaking hand, while he swiped at the blood running into his eyes. Behind him, I saw Paula's hand close around the darts lying on the desk. As Sonny steadied the gun on me, he growled, "You're dead!"

Suddenly Paula let out a bloodcurdling scream as her arm swung around in a wide arc. She struck Sonny in the side of his neck with the fist holding the darts. The force of the blow buried them in his flesh right up to the wood. A giant spurt of blood shot out his neck and the spray hit me in the face. Sonny dropped the gun and clutched at his throat. He pulled the darts out clumsily, but the wound continued to gush and spray. Based on the force and volume of the blood spurt, I knew she'd hit either the carotid artery or jugular vein. Sonny would bleed out before medical attention could do anything for him.

My ears were still ringing from the gunshot, and my shoulder was on fire. I was suddenly aware that the basement had filled with people and police. Diane was kneeling over me, crying, and I realized Sonny wasn't the only one bleeding out. Eddie Murphy and Gene Rame hurried over and knelt beside me. "Did you get it?" I asked them. Gene Rame nodded and smiled grimly. "We got it all. The wire picked up everything." Just before I passed out, I looked at Diane and said, "I guess Paula was right about those darts all along!"

CHAPTER THIRTY-THREE"

After Characters closed, Miguel closed down his operation as well. He told me that through the years he'd stashed over $750,000 in a safety deposit box and had sent an equal amount of money back home to Colombia. His family had been investing it for him there in real estate and had watched his investments grow. Miguel was going to retire a very wealthy man.

Mitzi went to prison for the money laundering. She was never officially implicated or charged in the disappearance/murder of Sal, and I doubt that will ever happen. The investigation is ongoing. but the lack of a body makes any resolution unlikely. Paula got what she wanted, to spend her retirement on an island. Unfortunately, it's Riker's Island.

I still suspect Diane of being complicit in, if not directly responsible for Old Man Eddie's "accident." There's no doubt in my mind that she followed Eddie to the subway station that Halloween night, with the intention of picking his pocket for the wallet they thought held Samantha's license. I don't want to believe Diane deliberately pushed Eddie to his death. With the crowd on the platform that night, he could easily have been jostled, or just lost his balance. Or maybe not. I guess I'll never know. I do know that with her pickpocket and lock picking skills, Diane's involvement in the whole business went deeper than she admitted to, but there wasn't enough evidence to build a case against her. Diane skated, free and clear. It was finally over.

Right from the beginning, it was all about people trying to manipulate other people. Sonny manipulating Paula. Sonny and Mitzi manipulating Sal. Diane manipulating Samantha. Samantha manipulating me… I didn't figure any of it out. I wish I could say I did, but I'm not that smart. No, I had the whole thing explained to me by Samantha, just before I killed her.

I'd shown up at her place that morning she hung up on me, right after Diane left. When Samantha met me at the door, she was holding a wet bloody towel to her head and was raging. She said that Diane had come over to ask her to drop the article she was working on. If she printed the story, Diane told her, Paula could end up going to jail. They fought, and Diane struck her. When she came to a few minutes later, Diane was gone.

I didn't understand. How could the stories about Characters land Paula in jail? She said she wasn't talking about my "stupid shit," but about something I knew nothing about. That's when she told me about the plan she and Diane had hatched to get the bar closed so Paula and Diane could retire to Florida. She laid it all out for me, every detail, in a malevolent, unhinged rant.

It got personal real fast. She told me I was nothing more than a stupid pawn, a dupe who was just being used right from the start to help them get what they wanted. She mocked me for believing she would ever need to resort to somebody like me for material.

She called me a cliché, just another coke-snorting, alcoholic fag. The story she was working on would get the bar closed permanently, she said, and I wouldn't even have my "shitty bartender job" when it was all over.

When I told her she couldn't do that, she laughed in my face. She said she could do any goddamn thing she wanted to, and I couldn't do shit about it. She told me if I got in her way she'd destroy me, and not to fuck with her! All she'd have to do, she said, is expose me as the source of all the stories she'd written.

And then she threatened me with the police. She told me that for my part in Miguel's drug sales, I could be arrested and charged with facilitating, and go to jail! Jail!! It won't be so bad, she sneered, saying a fag like me might actually enjoy jail. She laughed, and said it was bound to be preferable to the 'physical retribution' guaranteed to be coming my way after she outed me.

That's when I dispensed some physical retribution of my own. I hit her, hard. She fell to her knees, and I wrapped my hands around her throat and choked her. I choked her until I felt the fight go out of her — and then the life.

Not satisfied with that, and still wanting to hurt her, I picked up the ashtray and hit her some more. Feeling better, I got up and left the apartment, and, well, you know the rest. Sometimes I think about those people. I think about Sal, keeping Danny and Teddy Pope's dad company for eternity at the bottom of the East River. I think about Samantha, Diane, and Sonny, all thinking I was a nobody they could manipulate and use to their own ends.

I think about Old Man Eddie and wonder if he's pushing his wife around Heaven in a shopping cart. I think about him telling me, "There's an upside to being invisible to people, kiddo. They always underestimate you."

And I think about Tim Doherty, the exterminator, who said to me, "These people don't play by the same rules you live by, Billy. If you don't want to be the one who ends up in the hospital or the morgue, you have to get down and deal with them on the same level they're on. Otherwise, you're not going to…" What? Come out on top? Survive…?

THE END

ACKNOWLEDGEMENTS

I'd like to thank George Gilmore for giving me permission to use the quote from "Burnzy's Last Call," an independent film from 1995 that George authored. Also, a huge thanks to Marisa Perhaes Gorman for all her assistance to me during the course of this endeavor. Marisa, a retired Sergeant from the NYPD, has been a friend for longer than I care to say, and was there to answer any questions I had about police procedure and related matters, no matter how trivial, with insight and humor. Thank you, Reetza!

And of course my biggest thanks goes to my family: My cousins, George and Maureen Collins; my siblings, Michael, Doreen, and Judy Collins; my siblings-in-law, Michael's wife, the vivacious Molly Collins, and Doreen's current and final husband, Frank Vanacore; my nephew and niece, Sean and Devlin Healey; and my other brother in every way but blood, James Gallagher.

Their emotional, moral, and (sometimes) financial support has sustained me my entire life. I'm grateful and know how lucky I am to have them as family.

Finally, a special shout-out and tip of the hat to Jason Lynch, my friend and former co-worker from Boston, whose shenanigans involving a movie star and a gossip columnist sparked the inspiration for this book. Thanks Jason, and if I ever run into Rob Lowe, I've got a great story for him! Thank you, everybody!

And you might want to check out: "Burnzy's Last Call" is available on Amazon and for viewing on Hulu. If you're in the mood for another story about a New York bar, it's extremely entertaining and has a great cast!

"When I Was Blue" by Marisa Perhaes Gorman. Since her retirement from the police force, Marisa's written a terrific book about her years as a police officer in New York City. In a compelling read, she writes of the travails she faced as a woman in an organization rife with toxic masculinity – the NYPD. It's available on Amazon, and I highly recommend it.

Oh, wait — !

One last plug: My sister Doreen Collins also has a book out, titled *Confessions of A Working Girl, or, How to Get Laid (Off)!* Go to Amazon and check this out as well for a fast and extremely funny read. It's really good, and I'm not just saying that because I'm her brother. (Honest!)